# "I've been wanting to touch you so badly,"

Cameron whispered as his fingers traced the contours of Summer's breast. "You were made for my hand. See?"

She couldn't see because her eyes were shut tight against the pain of desire. Nor could she pull away or tell him to stop.

Cameron kept kissing her. His hand slid to her bottom, cupping the softness. *Trust me.* The words weren't said aloud, but Summer heard them nevertheless.

Through a haze of passion, she felt him unbutton her blouse, felt the cool air on her heated skin.

"Look, Summer," he urged aloud now.

Again she didn't want to look. She wasn't sure of herself . . . she wasn't like other women. She wanted to be Julia Roberts or Kim Basinger or any other alluring female. She wanted to be sexy. She wanted to be fulfilled. . . .

*I don't want Julia or Kim. I want you.*

W9-BEN-707

Dear Reader,

Temptation is Harlequin's boldest, most sensuous romance series . . . a series for the 1990s! Fast-paced, humorous, adventurous, these stories are about men and women falling in love—and making the ultimate commitment.

Nineteen ninety-two marks the debut of Rebels & Rogues, our yearlong salute to the Temptation hero. In these twelve exciting books—one a month—by popular authors, including Jayne Ann Krentz, Barbara Delinsky and JoAnn Ross, you'll meet men like Josh—who swore *never* to play the hero. Matt—a hard man to forget . . . an even *harder* man not to love. Cameron—a rogue *not* of this world. And Jake—a rebel *with* a cause.

Twelve rebels and rogues—men who are rough around the edges, but incredibly sexy. Men full of charm, yet ready to fight for the love of a very special woman. . . .

I hope you enjoy Rebels & Rogues, plus all the other terrific Temptation novels coming in 1992!

Warm regards,

Birgit Davis-Todd
Senior Editor

P.S. We love to hear from our readers!

# The Outsider
## BARBARA DELINSKY

## Harlequin Books

TORONTO • NEW YORK • LONDON
AMSTERDAM • PARIS • SYDNEY • HAMBURG
STOCKHOLM • ATHENS • TOKYO • MILAN
MADRID • WARSAW • BUDAPEST • AUCKLAND

If you purchased this book without a cover you should be aware
that this book is stolen property. It was reported as "unsold and
destroyed" to the publisher, and neither the author nor the
publisher has received any payment for this "stripped book."

Published March 1992

ISBN 0-373-25485-7

THE OUTSIDER

Copyright © 1992 by Barbara Delinsky. All rights reserved.
Except for use in any review, the reproduction or utilization
of this work in whole or in part in any form by any electronic,
mechanical or other means, now known or hereafter invented,
including xerography, photocopying and recording,
or in any information storage or retrieval system, is forbidden without
the permission of the publisher, Harlequin Enterprises Limited,
225 Duncan Mill Road, Don Mills, Ontario, Canada M3B 3K9.

All the characters in this book have no existence outside the
imagination of the author and have no relation whatsoever to
anyone bearing the same name or names. They are not even
distantly inspired by any individual known or unknown to the
author, and all incidents are pure invention.

® are Trademarks registered in the United States Patent and
Trademark Office and in other countries.

Printed in U.S.A.

# 1

THE STORM CAME from the south. It was predicted, but even if it hadn't been, Summer VanVorn would have sensed its approach. She didn't know why that was, whether a sudden drop in the barometric pressure affected her blood, but it had always been so. With the approach of a storm, she was inevitably out of sorts.

This one came up the Atlantic coast, her portable radio told her. It didn't touch land long enough to weaken, but created havoc on nearly every offshore island along the way.

The Isle of Pride was in its path, which was unusual enough to explain why Summer was taken off guard. Oh, she had felt it coming. She had experienced the faint vibrating inside, the ultrasensitivity to touch, the feverlike warmth of her skin, but she had been convinced that this hurricane, like so many before it, would veer off to sea and die well before it reached Maine.

Then again, perhaps she had convinced herself so because she had wanted it to be. August was when she sailed to VanVornland. Like Pride, VanVornland was an island, though an uninhabited one with not so much as the crudest dirt road or log cabin or stone wall. To Summer's knowledge, it wasn't on any map but was, rather, her family's secret. Particularly now that she was the last living VanVorn, the two weeks she spent there each year were a balm. Had it not been for mundane needs of the flesh, such as food, clothes and shelter when winter came, and the less mundane need to tend the meadow where the ponies of Pride grazed, she might have lived there year-round.

This time Summer should have left sooner. She knew it within an hour of setting sail for home. The sky grew progressively darker, and the vibrations inside her picked up along with the wind, such that before long her hands ached trying to hold in the sails. But she didn't allow for slack. Time was of the essence. Normally the trip from VanVornland to the Isle of Pride took eight hours. She was hoping to make it in six, which was about all she estimated she had before the storm hit in full.

Before another hour had passed, she realized that she had been overly optimistic. The storm was upon her, racing head-on beneath a swirl of angry clouds. She pulled a windbreaker over her jersey and shorts, plaited her long blond hair with elastic bands, tied down everything in sight and braced herself as the wind rose. In an attempt to protect herself from the spray of the sea, she sank lower in the boat. Still she was soaked to the skin before another hour had passed. She was also frightened. She had sailed in bad weather before, but never in weather like this. It was all she could do to hold the rudder steady and keep the sloop headed due west.

*Sail home, Summer, sail home,* she commanded. *The ponies are alone. They may need you.*

But no amount of determination and grit in a waif of a woman could counter the sheer force of the storm. When the rains came, colluding with the wind to churn the sea and whip the boat furiously about, she had no choice but to lower the sails. She huddled beneath them, intent on riding out the storm.

She didn't know how long she stayed there, wet and cold at the base of the mast while the boat rolled and heaved. When waves topped the gunwales and poured inside, she set one hand to bailing and held on for dear life with the other.

Then, with an ominous crack, the mast split in two, and her fear approached panic. The boat listed toward where the broken mast lay, drawing in water so quickly that bailing was absurd. Grabbing the cushion on which she'd been kneeling, she barely had time to thread her arms through its straps when a fierce wave knocked her to the floorboards. She felt a stab of pain, but it was forgotten in the next instant when, with a terrifying yawing sound, the boat reared up and arched over.

Summer was thrown clear. She sank in the chilly North Atlantic, emerging seconds later gasping and frantic. The hull of the boat lurched in the waves not far from her. She tried to reach it, but was beaten back, coughing, again and again until, as though taking pity on her, the sea gave her a backhanded toss toward the sloop.

She hit the wooden hull with a cruel thud. Ignoring a cutting pain, she hauled herself up on the keel. There she lay, with her head pressed to the wet wood, while the rain pelted her and the wind and the waves dared her to ease her hold for so much as a second. That was all it would take, she knew. One second, and she'd be lost.

*Hold on, Summer. Hold on.* She thought of the ponies in the meadow. She thought of the small cabin nearby, where her mother had raised her and where she still lived. She thought of the harpsichord and her flute and the small pipe she'd carved of reed, and she played the sweet music in her mind so that she wouldn't have to hear the roar of the wind and the waves.

Inevitably, she weakened. Her limbs grew numb from the cold and the strain of holding on, and the pain in her head and side worsened until breathing was an effort. Dizzy, she lost her grip. She clawed at the keel and regained it, but no sooner was she atop the boat when she felt herself slipping again. This time the world went white and silent. When she came to, the buoyant cushion was gone, she was flailing her way to the surface, then gasping for air, and her boat was nowhere in sight. She whirled around in the water but couldn't see it. She opened her mouth to cry out her anguish, only to have it filled with water before any sound emerged. She sank and surfaced choking, unable to get enough air.

Then something touched her. Too defined to be a whale or a dolphin, it flattened itself to her back, grasped her waist and hauled her to the surface. "Breathe," it yelled.

She fought, first against the arm that restrained her, then, when she realized the arm wouldn't drag her under again, for air.

The yelling went on, the voice male and strong. "That's it. A little at a time. You'll be all right now. You're safe." His legs worked behind hers, holding their heads above the waves.

"My boat!" she sputtered.

"Gone," he yelled. Shifting her to his back, he fastened her arms around his neck. "You'll have to hold on. Can you do that?"

She nodded against his head, suspecting that it was less a case of holding on as being unable to let go now that her arms were in place. More numb than ever, she lay limply while he began to swim.

Thoughts came in spurts. *How could he keep them afloat? How could he make progress against the sea? How did he know where to go? Where was his boat?*

She faded in and out, aware one minute, unaware the next. She knew she was trembling, but the sensation was distant. In fact, everything felt distant, even, now, the danger. She didn't know how he did it, but her rescuer was moving them steadily through the waves. He kept swimming without tiring, his body exuding equal amounts of purpose and strength. Totally depleted of the latter, Summer had no choice but to put her fate in his hands.

She was only semiconscious when she felt a change in the rhythm of his stroke. Forcing herself awake, she looked through the wind and rain to see massive dark boulders looming ahead. At nearly the same instant, her swimmer drew her around, lifted her in his arms and strode out of the water.

"I'm home!" she managed in astonishment. She didn't understand. She was sure that the Isle of Pride had been hours away from where the boat had overturned. "How did you . . . ?"

"We weren't as far away as you thought," he said in a voice that was deep and hoarse. He carried her across the ribbon-thin beach and set her down on the wet sand beneath the shelter of a granite overhang. The rain blew in, but his broad back and shoulders deflected it. He bent his head toward hers. "How do you feel?"

"Numb," she answered, but she was shaking in earnest.

He slid a wet hand under the dripping plait of her hair, curving it supportively to her neck. "You're in shock. You need to be warm and dry. Where do you live?"

Her teeth were chattering, though she wasn't aware of being cold. What she was aware of was that this man was a stranger and that she didn't have men, strange or otherwise, in her home. Ever. She didn't trust them.

But this one had saved her life. He couldn't be wholly evil. Besides, she wasn't sure she could make it home on her own.

In apprehensive bursts, she said, "I live up island. Fifteen minutes' walk. There's a path down the beach. It leads to a road."

The words were barely out when he lifted her in his arms again and set off. She knew he had to be dead tired and wondered where he found his strength. Without missing a step, he found the path and, holding her even closer to his chest to shield her from the storm, climbed it. At the road at the top, he leaned into the wind and headed home.

For the first time in her life, Summer wished one of the islanders would drive by. But the chances of that were next to nil. After battening down the hatches, they would be staying put until the storm passed. They had no reason to budge. After all, they didn't fear for the trees in the meadow where the ponies grazed. As far as they were concerned, the trees were simple beeches, easily come by, easily lost. Summer knew better. Those broad leaves contained critical nutrients. If the beeches went, the ponies were doomed.

Unable to even consider that possibility, she closed her eyes and focused on the man who carried her. His arms were strong, his hold oddly comforting. Knowing Pride's landscape like the back of her hand, she tracked his progress in her mind's eye. "There's a road ahead," she managed at one point, though it was an effort to make herself heard above the wind. "Go to the end. Then turn left."

The storm raged unabated. With unflagging stamina, he shouldered his way through it. Summer knew she should tell him to put her down, thank him, leave him and go on alone, but she didn't think she could walk. Pain was breaking through her numbness, most of it involving her knee. She had to tend to it, and for that she had to get home.

The instant he turned off the road and onto her path, she forced herself to full awareness. "Stop here. I have to check the meadow."

"Not now."

"But there may be damage."

"Until the storm stops, you can't do a thing. Besides, you're hurt."

She tried to deny it. "I'm all right. Really I am."

Ignoring her, he carried her up the cabin steps and inside. With the closing of the door on the storm, its cacophony was abruptly muted. Carefully, he set her down on the cushiony sofa. "First a fire," he said and turned to the large stone hearth.

Summer pushed herself up. Fighting a wave of dizziness and a harsh twinge in her middle, she tried to stand. Her knee screamed in pain, the sound echoing up through her throat. In an instant, the man was beside her, pressing her back. His voice was as gentle as his hands were firm.

"Please. Don't move until I've had a chance to see what's wrong." He took the wool afghan that had been folded over the sofa back and started to cover her but she pushed it quickly away.

"I'm too wet. It'll be soaked in a minute." She plucked at her clothes. "I have to get these off." Again she struggled up, this time aware of more pain. She tugged at the windbreaker, but her fingers were too shaky to undo much of anything. So he helped her. "No," she protested.

"You can't do it yourself."

"*You* can't do it."

"Why not?"

Before she could tell him that she was frightened, a wave of weakness engulfed her, preventing her from arguing.

Seeming fully aware that any movement would cause pain, he carefully eased the windbreaker over first one arm, then the other, then over her head. Her jersey followed, and Summer grabbed for the afghan. She had never been one to wear a bra, and it didn't matter that this man had saved her life, he was still a stranger. For all she knew, his idea of a neat vacation was sailing through hurricane winds, rescuing a damsel in distress, then ravishing her. She knew nothing about him but that he was large and as wet as she was.

He reached for the lamp.

"Won't work," she said as she struggled to wrap the afghan around her. "The electricity goes in a storm. Use the lantern by the stove." Breathing shallowly against the pain in her ribs, she lay down again. "Matches are beside it."

She closed her eyes and concentrated on controlling the pain. Seconds later, she felt a light beyond her lids and opened her eyes to see the stranger hunkering down before her. His face was lit by the glow of the lantern. It was a wet face, but a handsome one, with dark hair damp and spiked on his forehead, a straight nose, a square jaw and navy blue eyes that were filled with concern.

"Where does it hurt?" he asked.

"Everywhere," she moaned, thinking to make light of her injuries by gross exaggeration, except that the exaggeration wasn't gross. Her skin was a mass of needle pricks, and beneath it one bruise after another was springing to life.

He looked behind her, then at the open loft overhead. "Is that the only bed?"

"Yes."

"You'll be warmer here," he said and rose to his feet to return to the hearth. When he had a fire going, he came to sit by her hip. Gentle hands prodded her forehead.

"Hurt?" he asked. She nodded. "Do you have a head-ache?" Again she nodded. Then she caught a glimpse of his fingers.

"I'm bleeding?"

"Afraid so." He left her. She heard his footsteps on the wood floor, heard the open and close of cabinets first in the kitchen, then the bathroom. *You don't know him, Summer,* said a tiny voice in her head. *You can take care of yourself. You always have. Sit up. Make him leave.* But the voice was too tiny, too distant to be heeded. She turned her face toward the cushion, suddenly perva-sively tired, wanting only to sleep. Within seconds the cushion dipped, and the same gentle hands that had prodded her forehead were cleaning the cut there. She was too weak to wince at the antiseptic's sting.

He was a doctor, she decided. She had never been to one, but she'd heard enough about them to be sure of it. She didn't know how he had come to be in the ocean with her, but he seemed to know what he was doing.

Still, when he reached for the edge of the afghan, she clutched it to her.

"I want to help," he said in a low voice that seemed to seep into her body and soothe her. His eyes aided the gentling. They were direct, penetrating but kind. "You need tending, but you can't do it yourself. I won't harm you. I didn't carry you out of the ocean for that."

*He lies,* the tiny voice said, but the rest of her wouldn't listen. His voice felt so good, his eyes so sincere and his words so right that she didn't fight him this time when he reached for the afghan and drew it aside. She turned her head away, unable to watch, but she felt everything he did. His hands were large, warm and capable. They probed and pressed. They touched her with care, gently but persistently. Each time she gasped at the pain, his palm lay still on her for a minute. Each time, he waited for the pain to ease before resuming his examination.

"Looks like you've bruised some ribs," he finally said, then turned his attention to her hip. A tiny sound of protest was all she could manage before he had slipped down the band of her panties. "You must have hit something hard. The skin split in two." He took the cloth and antiseptic to the cut, then left her, this time to find gauze. By the time he returned, she had drawn the afghan over her breasts.

He worked on her hip for a bit, his touch careful and, in that, reassuring. She drifted off, only vaguely aware when he moved down to bathe a cut on her thigh. When he touched her knee, though, she twisted up in sudden, excruciating pain. Taking shallow gasps, she tried to catch her breath.

He pressed her down, massaging her temples so lightly that she began to float. He spoke softly; she couldn't make out the words but they soothed her while his fingers kneaded her skin. The knee didn't seem as painful when he returned to it, and she drifted off again.

When she awoke, it was dark outside. The wind was still up, slapping rain against the windows. As though to compensate, flames crackled in the hearth, sending forth a welcome warmth.

The stranger was sitting on the floor with his back against the sofa. His chest was bare, as were his feet, leaving his jeans, riding low on his hips, his only covering. The flames lit his face, but Summer had precious few seconds to study his profile before he turned his head and met her gaze.

"How do you feel?" he asked softly.

The voice and the eyes were as soothing as before, but the body frightened her. It was large, so large, and at ease enough in her home to make her nervous. His chest was broad, a muscled expanse whose hair-spattered skin reflected the glow of the fire—all of which made her aware that she was female and small, and at that moment pitifully weak.

He frowned. "I won't hurt you. Really, I won't."

She swallowed. Her gaze fell to his chest.

"My things were wet, too," he explained. "They were uncomfortable. I was cold."

She felt torn. The man had saved her life under the most heroic of circumstances, brought her safely home and ministered to her cuts and bruises. *Would* he hurt her after all that? Besides, there was something else, something about his face that was familiar. She tried to place it but couldn't, and decided that the familiarity came from having seen him before she'd slept.

"How do you feel?" he asked again.

Her voice was thin. "Like I've been stepped on by an elephant." Recalling the horror of the storm-tossed sea, she said, "But it's okay. I'm lucky to be here. Thank you for saving me."

He acknowledged her words with a small inclination of his head but otherwise made no move. "Is your forehead better?"

It still ached, but more dully than sharply. "Some."

"The ribs will be sore for a while. How's the knee?"

Remembering all too well how much it had hurt when he'd touched it, she resisted a test. "I broke something there, didn't I?"

"No. It's just a bad sprain."

She could have sworn there had been a break. She had never felt such sharp, centered pain in her life. Needing to know for sure, she tried moving her knee. The pain was still there, but it was nowhere near what it had been. She reached down to touch it, to prod much as he'd done earlier, and indeed the knee felt relatively benign. More disconcerting by far was the realization that she was wearing a nightgown and nothing else. That meant that this man who had saved her life, this man who was so physically superior to her, this man who seemed to have taken command of her home, had seen her stark naked. No man had ever seen her stark naked before.

One almost had. It had happened several years before on a foggy November day. She had been walking home from town, her arms filled with supplies, when she had been accosted. That man, too, had been larger and stronger than she, but his eyes had been filled with such lust as he tore at her clothing that he hadn't grasped her intent until her knee had found its mark. She had fled, then had sat in her cabin with a gun aimed at the door for the rest of the day and night. He hadn't come, and the following week he had died in an accident at sea. She hadn't been sorry. She had wished for his death. He'd been cruel. The world was better without people like him.

And this man? He had saved her life, and though he had undressed her, he hadn't hurt her or been cruel. In a shaky voice, she asked, "Who are you?" She remembered that his eyes were navy blue, though with the light of the fire behind him, she couldn't see their color just then.

"The name's Cameron," he said. "Cameron Divine."

It rang no bells, though the oddly familiar something about his face tugged at her again. "Where are you from?"

He tossed his head. "Up north."

A Canadian. They were common in Maine, particularly during the summer. If he was a regular visitor to Pride, she might well have passed him in town, which would explain the sense of familiarity she felt. "Have you been here before?"

"No."

So much for having seen him. "What were you doing in the ocean?"

A wry smile tugged at the corner of his mouth. "Same thing you were. Seems like this storm has a hunger for boats."

"You were sailing?"

He nodded.

"From one of the other islands?" There were hundreds along the coast.

"Uh-huh."

"All alone?"

He nodded again.

She studied his face and couldn't see a single blemish there, nor on his body. Her gaze traced corded sweeps of muscles that started at his shoulders and tapered to his wrists. She wondered how he'd come to be so beautifully built, and how he had managed to escape injury.

"I was fortunate," he said as though reading her mind. "I was tossed clear of my boat just before it shattered."

She remembered the way he had put her on his back and swum through miles of churning sea. She didn't care how well-toned he was. What he'd done had been superhuman. "How did you manage it?" she asked in amazement.

He shrugged and faced the flames. "I'm in good shape."

That was an understatement, she decided, and she was in a position to know. Just because no man had ever seen her naked didn't mean the reverse was true. She had seen plenty of naked men. Many a time when someone on Pride was sick or injured and conventional medicine wasn't helping, she was called in to do what she could with her poultices and balms. Granted, it usually happened under an aura of secrecy, in the dark of night so

that the rest of the town wouldn't know. Still she had seen
all there was to see of many an islander. She knew the in-
tricacies of the male body, certainly enough to know that
Cameron Divine's, bare above and gloved by damp jeans
below, was finer than any of those others.

"But through a *hurricane?*" she asked.

"It's a question of rhythm," he said with the small shift
of one of those firm shoulders. "I actually didn't do as
much swimming as you think. The waves carried us most
of the way."

She persisted. "But we didn't go under."

"I kept my lungs filled. That kept us afloat."

"But people don't survive what we did! We should
have drowned ten times over!"

Slowly he turned his head and met her gaze. *But we
didn't drown,* his eyes said in a definitive tone, *and that's
all that counts.* Aloud he said, "Would you like some
soup?"

She was so stunned by the eloquence of his eyes, that
it was a minute before the question sank in. She shot a
look at the stove, where her large pot sat.

"I put something on to cook while you were sleeping," he explained. "I don't know if it'll be any good. You
have some weird things in your cupboard."

Indeed she did, Summer mused, and the irony of that
hit her. Medicinal soups were her specialty, which was
why all those "weird things" were there. She knew just
what to boil into a broth to speed mending and restore
strength—but she was too weak to get up and make it,
which meant that her own insights were useless just when
she needed them most.

She wasn't about to tell Cameron all that. Typically,
those people who thought her fey gave her a wide berth,
while those who thought her possessed were less kind.
She didn't know which way Cameron would see her and

didn't care to test him until she was in a better position to defend herself.

Silently she watched him rise to his feet and stride toward the stove. He ladled steaming liquid into a cup, then returned to the sofa and helped her sit up. She held the cup beneath her nose and breathed in the vapors, breaking them down enough to identify which of those "weird things" he had dumped into the soup. With certain combinations, she could easily pass out, perk up, start vomiting, break into a sweat or sprout hair on her chest.

But no, he'd done all right, she decided and took a sip of the broth. She didn't detect anything that would hurt her. True, she might have added one or two different herbs to maximize the healing, but this was fine, actually quite good.

"Did I do okay?" he asked, again seeming aware of her thoughts.

Embarrassed by her transparency, she managed a smile. "You did."

He received the smile with a look in his eyes that fully rewarded it—and stunned her again. This time the surprise didn't come from silent words, but from feelings, specifically a tingling inside that sparked a strange warmth.

"Drink up," he urged softly and directed his gaze to the fire.

Summer drank, but as she did, she thought about that look and the one before that had spoken so clearly to her. He had spectacular eyes, Cameron Divine did. A spectacular body and spectacular eyes, both of which were remarkable observations coming from Summer Van-Vorn. She wasn't a connoisseur of men in the sexual sense. When she tended them, they were patients, period. She had never been touched, tempted or turned on, and she wasn't any of those things with Cameron

Divine, she assured herself. But there had been that odd warmth, which said that she was aware of him as a man, which was unsettling.

More unsettling, she was aware that he would be spending the night in her home and that she still knew precious little about him. So she asked, "Are you a doctor?"

He was in the chair by the fire, with his long legs stretched toward the heat. "No."

"What, then?"

"A research scientist."

That sounded very official and too complex for her to deal with just then. She was feeling sleepy again. "Where do you work?"

"A lab."

"Where?"

"Up north."

He had said the same thing before. She wished he would be more specific. Vagueness made her wonder what he was hiding—not that she knew much about Canada, anyway.

She sank deeper into the sofa. "Do you have family?"

He shook his head.

"None?" she asked. She wanted to think he had a loving wife and a bunch of loving children at home waiting for him. That would be as fine a character reference as any. When he shook his head again, she asked, "No one who'll worry you were lost at sea?"

"Not for a while." Which meant that he wasn't in any rush.

Her eyes drifted shut. If the man was evil, she was in trouble. Her cabin was isolated. He didn't look like he planned to leave. She couldn't force him out. Especially now. Because she felt strange. Muzzy. Drugged.

"I want—to go to—the loft," she said in a disjointed voice. Generating fragments of strength, she slid her feet to the floor and pushed herself to a sitting position. She had an arm wrapped around her ribs to minimize the pain there when Cameron squatted before her, blocking her way.

"You'll be warmer down here."

His face was swimming. "I have—to—go up."

Her urgency must have come across, because without further argument he slipped an arm under her shoulders and knees, lifted her and carried her toward the stairs.

"No need to carry me," she whispered against his chest, but she was fading fast and unable to help it. He had put something in the soup. He had to have. That was the only reason she could think of that she was slipping away. Fighting to preserve what little consciousness remained, she let him settle her under the quilt.

"Okay?" he asked, smoothing strands of hair from her face.

"Okay," she whispered. She waited for him to turn away, then couldn't wait any longer. Defying a dizzying daze, she reached into a drawer by the bed, took out a small black pistol and, with her finger on the trigger, at the ready should it be necessary, slid it under the pillow. Only then did she sink into oblivion.

# 2

THE GUN WAS GONE. Summer hadn't been awake for more than thirty seconds when she realized it. She was sure it had been in her hand when she'd fallen asleep, and though she wasn't immediately sure why it had been there, that didn't matter. Lying half on her side, half on her stomach, she groped around under the pillow, then under the quilt, when a deep voice said, "I have it. I was afraid you might shoot yourself in your sleep."

She gasped. Her head flew around, eyes focusing with some effort on the owner of the voice as the thudding of her heart sparked flashes of memory. Cameron. He was sitting on the floor not far from her bed, with his elbows propped casually on bent knees and his feet planted widely on the floor. He was still bare-chested and looked larger in the confines of the loft. The gun dangled from his hand.

"Why do you think I'd hurt you?" he asked, sounding mystified.

She tried to find an answer but was too frightened to think. The events of the night before were misty in her mind.

"I brought you safely from the sea," he pointed out as he had once before, she seemed to recall. "Why would I hurt you?"

She didn't know. She didn't understand men.

He held out the gun. "Here. Take it if it'll make you feel safer."

Without apology, she took the weapon and tucked it by her breast, then closed her eyes and tried to still the racing of her pulse.

After a minute, he asked, "Have you ever used it?"

*Of course,* she wanted to say. *I'm a fine shot. Come at me, buster, and you're a dead man.* But she wasn't good at lying, and besides, there was something about Cameron that discouraged it. How could she explain that she was a loner, that her experience with people, be they male or female, hadn't been largely positive?

"No," she confessed softly. "I've never used it."

"Then why do you have it?"

She met his gaze with what she hoped was subtle warning. "Because there's always a first time."

He didn't respond, simply looked at her with those dark blue eyes. They seemed nearly as deep as the sea, not stormy now but calm and hypnotic. Under their spell, she took one breath, then another longer, deeper one when the first seemed a balm.

More gently he asked, "How do you feel?"

She stretched gingerly. "Stiff."

"Are you in pain?"

"No, no pain." At least nothing sharp, she mused in relief. But there was a lingering lethargy that seemed to weigh down her limbs. She remembered how quickly it had come over her the night before. Memory crystalized, putting her on guard once again. "What did you put in my soup? Something knocked me out."

"You knocked yourself out. You had a busy day. You needed the sleep."

"What time is it?"

"Eleven."

*"Eleven."* She pushed herself up, ignoring twinges along the way. "I never sleep this late. It was the soup, I

know it was." She grew still, listening, then whispered, "The storm's over?"

"Pretty much. It's just raining now."

She should have known it the instant she'd awakened. Her skin wasn't as sensitive as it had been during the storm, her temperature felt normal, and even in spite of Cameron's disconcerting presence, she was calmer all over. Pushing the quilt aside, she swung her feet to the floor, but when she tried to stand, her knee buckled. She sat down fast and set both her hands and her mind to massaging it.

Cameron didn't move. "Where are you going so fast?"

"To the bathroom," she said, trying not to look at him. He was too large. He was too *strong*. By comparison, she felt small and weak, both of which she resented. "Then to see my ponies in the meadow."

"They're yours?"

"Well, yes. They don't belong to anyone else, and I'm the one who cares for them." She worked her hands over and around her kneecap, concentrating on finding every weak spot and strengthening it with her touch. She was still surprised that nothing was broken, given the pain she'd first felt. The muscles were bruised, but that was all.

"The ponies are wild, then?" Cameron asked.

"Yes."

"Strange," he mused after a pause. "I wouldn't have thought an island this far north could support a band of wild ponies."

The challenge in his voice drew her gaze to his. His eyes were deep and riveting, his face innocent, and, in that, more beautiful than she'd thought it the night before. *Trust me*, his look said. *Talk to me*. Though she fought it, the words touched her and shook her. She felt her breath catch in the back of her throat and had to force it on. Even then, the best she could manage was a slightly feeble, "Only in summer."

She wasn't used to having a man around, that was all, she told herself. She wasn't used to having a man in the cabin, much less in her bedroom, and Cameron's presence wasn't one to be ignored. She had to get dressed, had to get out, had to see how passable the island roads were. The sooner Cameron Divine was off Pride the better. She wanted things safe. She wanted them back the way they'd been. She wanted to be alone again.

Bearing her weight on her good leg, she rose to gingerly test the bad one. She had barely leaned onto it when Cameron was on his feet, bracing her elbow. "I'm okay," she assured him, cross with herself for the ailment.

"You're not," he argued. "That knee is still bruised. If you put weight on it now, you'll do more damage."

Needing to establish her independence, she shook off his hand. "I can walk," she insisted. Hobbling, she made her way down the stairs and into the bathroom. The minute the door was closed, she sank down on the edge of the tub to massage the bruise again.

"Defiance won't heal your knee!" Cameron called from just beyond the door.

"I'm not being defiant," she called back.

"Then stubborn!"

"Not that either. I'm *okay.*"

"Fine," he declared after a minute's silence. "If you want to bite off your tongue to spite your teeth, go ahead!"

FIFTEEN MINUTES LATER, Summer emerged from the bathroom feeling more like herself. She was wearing a clean pair of jeans and an oversize shirt, and had braided her hair and put medicine on her bruises. They were healing remarkably well. She had to admit that except for slipping something into her soup to put her to sleep, Cameron Divine had done all right.

Not that the sleep had hurt her. In fact, it had probably been for the best. Only it hadn't been Cameron's decision to make. Summer ruled her own life. She decided what she did and when. She didn't trust that anyone else could make those decisions quite as well as she could.

Telling herself that, she limped through the living room. Ignoring Cameron's presence at the hearth, she stepped into a pair of rubber boots, took her slicker from the hook by the door and left. Yes, her knee hurt. So did her ribs and her head. And yes, she knew that she would be best off staying in bed, but she couldn't afford that luxury. She had to recapture some small peace of mind, and for that she had to get to the meadow.

Pulling the slicker's hood over her head against a steady rain, she hobbled up the slope behind the cabin. The tall grass was slick underfoot. She slipped once, then again, each time catching herself with a hand on the ground, each time cursing the pain elsewhere. At the crest of the hill, the path leveled. She followed it, limping under an umbrella of pines, over a carpet of needles far thicker than what had been before the storm. The wind had clearly left its mark. In addition to those needles, there were fallen branches strewn around. She sidestepped some and moved others away. More housekeeping would be necessary, she knew, but later. Her first priority was reaching the meadow.

Then, with the sudden falling off of the pines, she was there and, for the first time in better than a day, she felt true hope. A thick fog hung over the rolling acreage. As her eyes adjusted, she made out shapes, and as those shapes sensed her presence and one by one approached, a slow smile softened her lips. She put her arms up to the first of the pale gray ponies, hugging its sleek neck, pressing her face to its ashen mane and inhaling the sweet blend of animal and woods. Her hood fell back, but the rain was suddenly more gentle, cleansing the horror of the storm. She reached out to touch another pony, then another until she had connected with each. By that time, her eyes brimmed with tears of happiness.

The ponies were fine. Not a one was missing, not a one injured. Nor were the beeches damaged, she realized as she limped around the meadow. The few leaves that had been lost would hardly be missed.

A damp nose nudged her hand. It was Pumpkin, so named not because he resembled a squash, but because he was so sweet and gentle that the moniker simply fit. He was the smallest of the ponies and the most cuddly. "Hello, sweetheart," she cooed, rubbing the wet velvet of his nose. "You did just fine, didn't you?" He slid his muzzle over her shoulder, encouraging a hug that she was all too happy to give. "I was so worried," she whispered tearfully. She held him tightly for a minute before planting a kiss on his neck. When she stepped back and continued her tour of the meadow, he stayed by her side. She fancied that he had noticed her limp and was concerned, for he waited until she had reached the head of the meadow and eased herself down on the large pine stump there before ambling away.

Taking a deep breath—carefully, so that she didn't put strain on her ribs—she let it out in a sigh of relief. This was her world. She felt safe here, loved here. If ever she'd known a peaceful spot, this was it. Slowly, as the rain misted the landscape, the fog gave shape to the air and the ponies grazed on the beech leaves, her tension began to seep away.

Reaching behind her, she drew her reed pipe from a hidden notch in the stump and started to play. The notes were soft and slow, mellow, almost haunted. In a cathartic flow, they spoke of what she had been through, what she had felt and was feeling now. Each note was new, never heard before, never to be heard again, and, in that, sad, for even to her own ear the notes were exquisitely beautiful. They worked their magic, soothing her body and soul as nothing else could.

So caught up was she in the sounds of the pipe that she didn't hear Cameron's approach. Suddenly feeling his presence, she whirled to find him barely an arm's length away.

"Don't stop," he urged. "That was lovely."

But Summer didn't play for people, so she was unable to return the pipe to her lips. She wanted to tell him that this was her meadow and that he was an intruder and should leave, but she was unable to do that either, because his dark blue eyes were saying, *I mean it, I do like your music.* He had to, she decided, or he'd turn and leave on his own. It was raining, and he had no coat. He was wearing the same jeans as before, along with his shirt and sneakers, and if the latter two had dried overnight, they were soaked again, but he didn't seem to notice. He didn't look bothered or uncomfortable or chilled. Rather, he looked perfectly at ease.

He was either devil or angel. She didn't know which.

Confused and unsure, she turned to the ponies. Pumpkin was ambling up, casting the occasional woeful glance at Cameron. He pushed his nose into her hand in a bid for reassurance.

"So these are your ponies?" Cameron asked.

Summer nodded.

"Are they really wild?"

Again she nodded. She didn't want to speak, didn't want to give him any encouragement to stay. Besides, it was easier not looking at him. His eyes talked to her in a way that was eerie.

His voice continued to come through the patter of the rain. "You said they were here only in summer. Where are they the rest of the year?"

"I don't know." She brushed at Pumpkin's forelock. Touching the pony gave her comfort.

"How can you not know?"

"I don't follow them when they leave."

"But if you care about them as much as you seem to, I'd think you'd want to know everything about them."

"No one knows everything about them," she said, responding to the challenge in his voice. "They swim ashore at the time of the summer solstice and leave when autumn begins. It's assumed that they island-hop until they get to the mainland, but what they do from there is a mystery. All I know is that they come back here year after year."

"To feed on these leaves?"

She nodded. "There's something special in them."

"What is it?"

She hesitated. The leaves, the ponies, the meadow were her business, not Cameron's. But he seemed genuinely interested. Most people weren't. So she said, "I don't know. I've tried to find out." Only to meet with frustration. "I've brought samples to labs on the mainland more than once, but no one has ever been able to isolate anything that isn't in beech trees everywhere else." They thought she was a crackpot for insisting there was. "But the ponies won't eat just any old beech leaves. I've brought them leaves from beech trees on the mainland,

and they won't touch them. These trees are different. I know they are."

She glanced at Cameron, expecting to find derision on his face, which was what she most often found when she talked about her ponies and the meadow. People thought she was daffy. But Cameron was hunkered down by her side, studying the ponies with a thoughtful look on his face. Unfortunately, that thoughtful look didn't hold her for long. Her gaze was lured downward by his wet shirt, which was molded to him like a second skin, outlining the muscles of his shoulders and back so vividly that he might as well have been bare-chested. She remembered when he had been just that, and felt the same tiny flare of warmth she had then. This time it was centered in the pit of her stomach.

When he suddenly looked back, catching her eye, she couldn't glance away. "Is this the only place the ponies graze?" he asked.

"Yes," she answered in a breathy voice that settled some as she spoke. "I've tried to lead them to other spots on the island, but they refuse to eat. Same thing when I bring in commercial feed or other kinds of grasses. They won't have any part of it."

"Why should they, if they have these trees?"

"Because someday they may *not* have them."

He frowned. "You mean, the trees might be wiped out in one full swap?"

She frowned back.

"Fell swoop," he corrected himself. "One fell swoop. Do you think that might happen?"

"It's possible. You saw what happened yesterday. Hurricanes come. This one didn't cause much damage, but the next one could." Her mother had been convinced that it would. She had warned of it more than once, the last time shortly before she had died. "Natural catastrophes happen. So do man-made ones."

"Man-made ones?"

"Like commercial development. Ever since I can remember, there have been people coming to look at this meadow with a thought to developing it somehow. One man wanted to put a resort here, another wanted to put a nine-hole golf course here, another wanted to build a retirement community here. In any of those cases, they'd have chopped down the beech trees to widen the meadow. They wouldn't have cared a whit about the ponies. They'd have simply let them show up here one summer and starve."

"I take it you told them that."

"I certainly did," she announced with a defiant tilt to her chin.

He grinned. "Good for you. Obviously, you talked them out of it, if they're not here now."

She gave Pumpkin a pat and watched him join the pack. "I don't know if it was my arguments that changed their minds."

"If not your arguments, then what?"

She shrugged. "Little things. The weather. The way puddles form here. The worms."

He eyed the ground between his sodden sneakers. "I don't see any worms."

"Snakes, actually," she said because it suddenly occurred to her that she'd been taking the wrong approach. She'd been trying to convince Cameron that she was like other people on the theory that he would be kinder to her if he didn't think she was odd. But she wanted him to leave, enough so that she was willing to risk his scorn just to scare him off.

"Snakes?" he asked.

"Big, thick, long ones," she said, careful to keep the drama of it at a plausible level. "There are times when the meadow is full of them."

He remained hunkered down, peering through the rain for sign of something big, thick and long. "I don't see any snakes here now."

She couldn't tell if he was uneasy. He might have no problem with snakes. "They only come when the meadow is in danger. Same with the bugs."

He raised a skeptical brow. "Bugs?"

"Uh-huh. They're like oversize mosquitoes, big and black with a buzz that drives sane people mad. When they start biting, they're relentless."

He stood then and tucked his hands into the back of his jeans. Still, she couldn't decide if he was put off, since there were clearly no mosquitoes there then. "So you get snakes and bugs." He mulled that over. "Do they bother the ponies?"

She shook her head.

"Just prospective plunderers of the meadow."

She nodded.

"You mentioned puddles. What about them?"

"They're huge. The place gets to looking like a pond."

"Doesn't look like a pond now."

"Because you're not threatening the meadow. But believe me, the ground floods, and when it floods, it *smells*. You could die from the smell, it's so bad sometimes. The townspeople swear up and down that the meadow is normally dry as a rock, but when buyers see those puddles and breathe in that stench, they envision all sorts of problems and get scared."

Cameron rubbed the back of his neck. "Naturally it rains whenever prospective buyers come."

"Or is humid enough to bring out the mosquitoes."

"Or the snakes."

"Uh-huh. This is a weird place," she said with just the right amount of warning. "Most island people think it's haunted."

Cameron looked at her. "Yet you stay. Do you think it's haunted?"

She made pretense of considering that before nodding.

"Aren't you frightened?" he asked.

She shook her head, looked him straight in the eye and said in an ominous tone, "I'm part of what's haunted. I'm the one who makes the snakes come, and the bugs and the puddles."

He laughed.

"You don't believe me?" she asked.

His eyes danced. "If you had that kind of power, you'd have long since conjured up something to scare me off."

"The only reason I haven't," she said, chagrined at having been seen through so easily, "is because you saved my life." Slipping the pipe into its sleeve in the tree stump, she stood and in the same movement started off — but without bracing her knee for the strain or herself for the pain. The knee gave, nearly toppling her. With a cry of dismay, she bent over it, but before she could do more than gird it with her hands, Cameron had lifted her into his arms.

"Put me down," she ordered, but she was concentrating too hard on soothing her knee to put up much of a struggle.

"Listen to reason," he said as he carried her toward the path. "You've injured your knee. I don't care what special powers you have, that knee needs rest."

She was remembering the other time when she'd been taken into the woods against her will. "Put me down!"

"When we reach your cabin."

"Now!" Frightened, she twisted in his arms, only to have them tighten around her. "Let me go!"

"Soon."

"*Let me go!*" Freeing a frantic arm, she struck out at his face.

"Hey," he yelled and tried to avoid her fist. It landed on his ear. "Whoa, hold it!"

She struck again, at the same time squirming every which way she could. She felt his arms loosen, felt herself starting to fall and being caught up again much as she'd been caught up in the ocean the day before. Only this time her back came to rest on the forest floor and Cameron's large body was pinning her to a bed of wet pine needles. She started to shake, not from shock or cold, but from stark terror.

"Hey," he repeated, but softly this time, and the eyes that scanned her face were puzzled. "Hey," he said again, as though he wasn't sure what else to do. *I won't hurt you. Why so frightened? I mean you no harm.*

Putting her soul into her own eyes, she begged him to let her go.

While he didn't quite do that, he rolled off her and drew her into his arms in a way that was far less threatening than the other. He held her like that, just held her, murmuring another, "Hey," every so often. Only when her trembling began to ebb did he ask, "What happened to you?"

She took a minute to catch her breath and in the aftermath of that terrified moment saw no cause to lie. "I was almost raped once. When I feel overpowered, it comes back."

He shifted her in his arms—didn't release her, but held her more gently against his chest, his breath mingling with the drizzle to warm her wet brow. "I won't rape you."

"Said the spider to the fly."

"Excuse me?"

She gave a tiny headshake.

"Do I look like a rapist?" he asked in a patient voice.

She didn't have to look. She had already done that enough to imprint his image boldly on her brain. "You're large and wet and dark," she said, but he didn't *feel* like a rapist. His arms were carefully placed so as not to hurt her where she was bruised and his body was more protective than menacing. Without deliberate intent, she felt herself giving him more of her weight.

"Are all rapists large and wet and dark?" he asked in the same quiet voice.

"No."

"Are all men rapists?"

"They have the ability."

"But the inclination?"

"How do I know? How do I know what goes on in men's minds?"

"Do you *think* all men believe in rape?"

She recalled the books and television shows she had listened to and was forced to admit, "No."

"Then why do you assume that I mean you harm?"

"Because," she said with her cheek to his chest, "the way you came out of nowhere in the middle of the ocean and carried me all the way to shore is scary. Now you're hanging around like you have nowhere better to go, and I'm not used to having anyone around, much less a man. You have to leave. I can't have you here."

"Because I make you nervous?"

"Because I don't want *anyone* here. You saved my life, and I'm grateful for that. But you can leave now. I'll do just fine."

"I'm sure you will," he said, but rather than setting her down and taking off for the center of town and a room at the inn, he rose with her in his arms and started down the path again.

"Did you hear what I said?" she asked, tipping her head to see his face.

"I heard." He kept walking.

"Well?"

"Well what?"

"You can leave."

He kept walking.

"Cameron?"

"I saved your life. You've said that more than once. The least you can do is let me break fast—uh, have break-fast."

"It's too late for breakfast."

"Lunch, then."

"Will you leave after that?"

He spared her a glance. *We'll see,* his eyes said, and she should have been scared out of her wits, but his hold was working its magic on her, making her feel comfortable and safe—and cared for, which was the strangest part of it. The only person who had ever cared for her had been her mother, and when she had died, Summer had thought that experience over and done. True, her mother had said there would be a man one day, but Summer hadn't believed her for a minute. All the men she had known were either distant or cruel. She couldn't imagine trusting one for long, not even Cameron.

"Here we go," he said a short time later when he carried her into the cabin and out of the rain. He set her carefully on her feet by the door and went for towels while she took off her slicker and stepped out of her boots. She limped past him on the way to the bathroom, took the towel he handed her and began to mop her face and hair. Once behind the closed door, she replaced her jeans with a pair of shorts, hung the jeans to dry and returned to the kitchen.

A towel-dried, shirtless and shoeless Cameron was at work at the stove. She didn't stop to ask what he was making, didn't want to know, didn't want to think about what could happen if he refused to leave. If he wanted lunch, he could help himself. She had work of her own to do.

Careful to avoid making contact with him, she gathered various herbs, leaves and powders from canisters and jars, mixed them in a pot with bits of liquid from assorted vials, and heated it. When that was done, she carried the pot to the table, sat on one chair with her knee on another and applied the steaming doughlike mixture liberally to the joint. Only when the whole thing had been sealed in with a hot towel did she sit back in the chair and let out a sigh.

"Better?" Cameron asked. He was leaning against the kitchen sink watching her, looking broader than ever with his arms crossed over his chest.

"Oh, yes." She could feel the vapors penetrating her skin, relaxing her muscles, soothing the ache.

"Where did you learn to do that?"

"Make poultices? My mother taught me."

"Was she a nurse?"

"No. She was a healer." Summer paused, then threw in, "Like me," and waited to see the derision on his face. But it never came.

"A healer," he mused. "I didn't know healers still practiced in modern societies."

"We do. Some think us to be witches." Again she waited for the power of suggestion to do its thing. But Cameron remained thoughtful.

"Is it a mind force you use, or natural things like what you put in that pot?"

"Natural things mostly." She had never been quite convinced of the other. Her mother had had it, had been able to think ailments better, and her grandmother even more so. But the ability had been diluted with each successive generation, leaving Summer to rely on what natural ingredients she gathered in the woods.

"And they work?"

"Usually."

He looked intrigued. "How did your mother learn the skill?"

"From my grandmother."

"How did your grandmother learn it?"

"From my great-grandmother."

"They were all healers?"

"Yes."

"And the men in the family, what were they?"

"Beats me," Summer said, holding his gaze with yet another challenge. "They never stayed around long enough to be much of anything but sweet talkers. They came briefly, made a baby and left. I'm as illegitimate as they come."

"You never knew your father?"

She shook her head.

"Never had any brothers or sisters?"

Just as she shook her head again, she thought she saw a flicker of anger cross his face. *I'm sorry,* his eyes said. *It shouldn't have been that way.*

"I've done just fine," she said with a touch of pride. "Some people are destined to live alone. I'm one of them."

"It shouldn't have been that way," he said aloud, and it was odd the way it came out, as though she was part of a master plan that had gone awry. "You're too pretty to live alone. Too gentle. Too vulnerable."

She scowled, wondering if this was the kind of sweet talking her mother had mentioned. If so, she was determined to resist. "I'm not vulnerable," she declared.

"You are. I see it in your eyes. And I hear it in your music." He looked beyond her to the harpsichord that stood in a corner of the living room. Crossing to it, he put a single hand on the keyboard and picked out the tune she had played for the ponies that day. The notes flowed with the same mellow timbre, the same haunted resonance, the same lilt of vulnerability that had come from her pipe. He played it a second time, so engrossed with the sound that he didn't see the shocked expression on Summer's face until the last of the tones had died, and by then it was too late. By then Summer knew that Cameron Divine was special.

# 3

HIS MUSIC SPOKE TO HER, echoing thoughts she'd had and feelings she'd known. Summer had been listening to music all her life, but it had never spoken to her quite this way before. Like the bottomless blue of his eyes, Cameron's touch connected with something deep inside her.

"How did you do that?" she asked in astonishment.

"Hmm?" Leaving the harpsichord, he approached her.

"How did you play that?"

"The harpsichord?"

"My song. That was what I played today in the meadow, but I don't know how you could remember it, or reproduce it that way." She couldn't have done it herself. Yet not only had he gotten the notes right, but he had injected the same emotion in them that she had. He had echoed her heart. She didn't understand.

Nonchalantly he proceeded to the kitchen counter. "I have an ear for music."

"Have you studied it?" she asked, watching the flex of his shoulders—beautifully tanned, she noted—as he reached for a pair of plates.

"Not formally."

"Informally?"

After a long minute of fussing with whatever he was making, he said, "I know music like you know healing. It was passed to me from my father, who got it from his father before him, and so on."

"What instruments do you play?" She was sure that he played the piano and suspected he played more.

He returned carrying two plates. "Whatever. I fool around with things. Actually, I've never played the harpsichord before." He set one of the plates before her and sat down with the other. "But I've always wanted to. It has a wonderful sound." He grew pensive, searching for words. "It's light, delicate—" his eyes brightened "—elegant."

Summer wouldn't have pegged him for the musical type. With his sturdy, bronzed body, he looked too physical for that. Yet not only was he musical, but he was musical in the same way that her own relatives had been. He could listen and reproduce, and reproduce with feeling. He could put his hands on an instrument for the very first time and coax something heartfelt from it. That was a gift.

Unsure of what to say, she dropped her gaze to the plate he'd set before her, then did a double take. Whatever Cameron had been busily preparing looked like nothing she had eaten before. Recalling the soup that had put her promptly to sleep, she asked, "What is this?"

"It's an open-faced sandwich," he said as though it was the most obvious thing in the world.

"But what's it made of?"

"Whatever I could find. There wasn't much in your icebox. I had to use what was in the cupboards."

She shot him a dubious look. "What exactly was that?"

"Brown bread from a can. Peanut butter, chocolate bits, peas."

She had recognized the chocolate bits but not the peas, which were mashed into a green paste and mounded over the peanut butter. "And what's on top?"

"Maple syrup."

That was what she thought. She gave the sandwich a nudge. "Interesting combination."

"I agree," he said, sounding proud of himself. "Mind if I start? I'm so hungry I could eat a house. Uh, horse."

"Go ahead." She sat back and watched him lift a round of brown bread and take a hearty bite of the concoction.

"Not bad," he said and took another bite. When the round was gone, he decided, "Not bad at all," and reached for a second.

Summer exchanged her plate with his. "You take my two. I'll finish up your one. I'm not all that hungry."

"Afraid I put something in yours that I didn't put in mine?" he asked with a grin that should have annoyed her, but instead drew her attention to the squareness of his chin and the stubble growing over his jaw. With his navy eyes teasing her, she felt a humming inside.

She prayed that the humming was from hunger and shrugged off his suggestion, though it wasn't totally bizarre. He wouldn't be the first man to charm a woman, then stab her in the back. "If so, we'll know soon enough." She watched him down another sandwich round with utter confidence and ease. His eyelids didn't suddenly sag, nor did he keel over. *Did you really expect that anyone who can play your music would be capable of poisoning you?* she asked herself dryly.

Out of curiosity, if not hunger, she took a bite of her sandwich and found that Cameron was right. The combination was surprisingly palatable. "Where did you learn to cook?" she asked.

He shrugged. "Wherever."

"Another skill handed from father to son?"

"I guess. But I'm not sure skill is involved when a person is hungry. What is it they say—necessity is the mother of convention?"

"Invention. Mother of invention." Summer regarded him quizzically. "You have trouble with those, don't you?"

"With what?"

"Idioms. I'll bet you mess up the punch lines of jokes, too."

He chuckled, never quite giving her an answer, and as she studied him, she forgot the question. His looks captivated her, driving all thought from her mind but that he was the most handsome man she had ever seen. If anything, the fact that he had trouble with idioms and probably messed up the punch lines of jokes made him all the more appealing. It made him fallible, humanly so, and that was reassuring, because, looked at in a certain light, she could almost imagine him otherwordly.

"Who are you?" she asked helplessly. "Where are you from?"

"Would you believe a distant planet?"

"No. Why are you here with me?"

He licked maple syrup from his fingertips. "I'm here because my sailboat was lost in the storm and along with it my money, my charge cards and my clothes. In a word, I'm totally, if temporarily, without resources."

Money, charge cards and clothes were very much earthly goods, she decided in relief. "Charge cards can be replaced. All it takes is a phone call."

"But you have no phone."

"There are phones in town."

"Would you send me out in the rain again, when I'm just now finally drying off?"

She looked for something threatening in his eyes, something to suggest that he was planning to take advantage of her, but his eyes were clear and direct. *Trust me*, they said and not for the first time. "But it could rain for days. That's what happens sometimes after storms like this one."

"It won't. The sun will be shining tomorrow."

"How do you know?" she challenged. *She* knew; the flow of her blood had a good-weather feel to it. But if Cameron Divine knew, she wanted to know how.

"The last weather report I heard before my radio went dead said something about the storm being powerful but compact, which means it came on relatively quickly and should end the same way. Believe me. The sun will be shining tomorrow."

She did believe him, and it wasn't only because her own body agreed. It was because he hadn't yet led her wrong. He had saved her from drowning, had returned her safely to her own home, had minimized wear and tear on her knee by carrying her around, had even made a lunch that, while unconventional, was nourishing and remarkably good. And he played her music.

After all that, could she really send him out in the rain?

Confused about how to stay on her guard when he was so appealing, she searched for a distraction in the towel circling her knee. Its heat was nearly gone. She began to unwrap it, but before she knew what he was about, Cameron had taken it from her and was heating it under the kitchen faucet. He wrung it out and brought it back, wrapping it around her knee himself this time. When the ends were secured, he settled his long frame into his chair. He didn't say anything, but she knew that he knew what she was thinking.

"I'm uncomfortable with this," she finally acknowledged, keeping her eyes on her knee.

His voice was quiet. "Yes."

"I'm not used to having anyone here with me."

"How long has it been since your mother died?"

"Nearly ten years."

"How old were you?"

"Eighteen. Before then, it was only the two of us, and since, it's been just me. You're the first person to sit at my table since she died. It feels strange." She remembered when her mother had been alive and the fun they'd had. There were times when she missed her terribly, other times when that companionship was so distant it might never have been. Life had gone on. "I'm set in my ways. I live alone by choice. I don't know what to do with other people."

"You're doing just fine with me."

"That's because you saved my life," she reasoned without looking up. "But I'm not a social person." When he didn't respond, she wondered if he was missing her point. Frustrated and more than a little embarrassed, she resorted to bluntness. "I'm not used to men."

"Have you ever been with one?" he asked without missing a beat.

Her eyes flew up, met his in a fleeting instant of sexual awareness, then lowered again. She felt her cheeks warm and was as disconcerted by the reaction as she was helpless to curb it. She had been with men—as in under the same roof—in the luncheonette and the grocery store, in private homes when she was summoned to treat someone ill or hurt and in numerous other locations. But she had never been with a man in bed. Given her age and the times, she was an anomaly.

Cameron was going to think her strange, and that suited the part of Summer that distrusted him and wanted him gone. The other part, the part of her that thought him special and was driven to know more about him, wanted his understanding.

With her eyes averted, she tried to explain. "I'm different from most women. I always have been. I was born in this cabin and raised here. My mother was nursemaid, teacher, doctor, playmate and confidante. I never went to school, because everything I needed to know I learned here."

"What about playing with other children?"

Her expression hardened. She wanted understanding, not pity. "You've never lived on an island like this, or you wouldn't be asking that question. The Isle of Pride supports a year-round population of eight hundred people—eight hundred people, most of whom are fishermen, and if they're not fishermen, they provide services for the fishermen. There is one school, one church, one main street, one general store. Everyone knows everything about everyone else. Mention the names Homesy, Dubay and Twill, and you're talking about generations of lobstermen. The Dunkirks are churchmen, the Shaws plumbers, the Thanes roofers." She paused. "The VanVorns are healers, and everyone knows that healers are strange. Island children steer clear of VanVorns. We're not thought to be normal, and that's fine," she hastened to add, "because I don't regret a thing. I lead a full, satisfied life. I've never been bored, not once. There's always something to do."

"Like what?"

"Like listen to music. Or watch television. Or sit with the ponies in the meadow. Or wash clothes, or gather herbs or leaves or bark from trees in the forest. Or garden—I grow most of what I eat. The growing season is short, so everything has to be planted, tended and harvested on schedule. Even now, next winter's supply of vegetables is out back waiting to be picked, cleaned and canned."

"Were the peas we just ate your own?"

She nodded. "Last year's. We'd have had fresh things if I hadn't been gone for the past two weeks." She applied a light pressure to the poultice, praying that her knee would heal quickly, what with all there was to be done.

"You didn't answer my question about men," Cameron said.

She evaded it still. "I don't have much opportunity to meet off-islanders. I've been to the mainland, but only a handful of times, and then only when I absolutely had to."

"Like when you took the beech leaves to the lab?"

She nodded.

"You can get everything you need, supplies and all, right here?"

"My needs aren't great."

"How do you support yourself? I mean, how do you pay for things? What source of income do you have?"

Her distrust reared its head. His questions were pointed ones, given that Cameron had no immediate resources of his own. "What source of income do *you* have?" she threw right back.

"I told you. I do research." Barely pausing for a breath, he asked, "Are you paid when you treat people?" *I'm curious*, his eyes said. *I won't rob you any more than I'd rape you, but you fascinate me. I've never known anyone like you before.*

She imagined she heard admiration in the words. Then it struck her that that was what she *wanted* to hear, and though she cautioned herself against falling for a handsome face and a sympathetic ear, she said, "Sometimes I'm paid. Sometimes I'm given goods in exchange for my services."

"And gratitude?" he asked insightfully. "Do you get that?"

She pursed her lips. "Sometimes."

"Only sometimes?"

"Like I said, healers aren't the most popular people around."

"You don't have to be popular to be given gratitude when you perform a service."

"Well," she replied, turning her attention to her knee, "that's neither here nor there. I don't live for the gratitude of the islanders." She unwrapped the towel, which had cooled again. "If they give it, fine. If they don't, that's fine, too. I go my way, and they go theirs. The less our paths cross, the better."

"Let me see that," Cameron said, suddenly towering over her. Setting the poultice on the table, he hunkered down to gently prod her knee. "How does it feel?"

"Okay," she said, but she had to concentrate on thinking about her knee with Cameron so bare, so near.

"Sore?"

"A little."

Very carefully, he moved her leg to further test the knee. It felt better than it had earlier, Summer decided with renewed faith in her skills. In the next instant, her skills were put to shame, though, for Cameron began a massage the likes of which she had never experienced before.

His hands flowed, surprisingly fluid for their size. She watched them for a time, trying in vain to decipher the pattern of their movements. "What are you doing?" she finally asked.

"Feel good?"

"Oh, yes," she admitted because anything that good had to be acknowledged. "But I can't figure out what's happening." It was as though he was taking her knee apart, setting aside skin, then muscle, then cartilage and bone, gently kneading each element as he went.

"It's nothing, really," he murmured, brows knitted as he concentrated on his work. "I know how the knee is made, so I know where to touch."

"I know how it's made, too," she argued, because her skill as a healer depended on that, "but I can't make it feel the way you do."

"That's because you're not me."

Summer felt a catch in the area of her heart. It was a simple statement, obvious and unpretentious, but it made her think of the way he had rescued her from the sea, ministered to her ailments, then played her harpsichord. Something was very different about Cameron Divine, she decided with even greater conviction, and it went well beyond the fact that he was male to her female. He was like no man she'd either heard of, seen on television or met. If he was a con artist, he was the best. She had to know more about him.

"You say you're a research scientist," she ventured, but in a soft voice because his touch, which had already reduced her knee to smooth jam, was conspiring with the warmth of his body to gentle the rest of her. "Is that where you learned about things like knees?"

"Yup."

"Do you work in Montreal?"

"North of there."

"How did you get here?"

"To the Maine coast? I flew. Then I rented a boat." He snickered. "Hope it was insured. It's history now."

"You were just off sailing by yourself?"

"Just off sailing by myself."

"For how long?"

"Before the storm hit? Three days."

"Do you sail a lot?"

"Nah. It's a pretty new hobby. I was loving it, even when things got wild out there, until the boat broke up. I didn't love it so much then." There was a dryness to his words, an edge that held more by way of amusement than upset.

"Won't someone worry?"

"About me?" He shook his head. "No one back home thinks twice when I take off for weeks at a stretch. I'm the universe's most ardent traveler. I do it a lot. So they're used to it. Months and they might worry, but a few weeks? Nope."

*You can't stay here,* Summer's mind screamed, but the words wouldn't form on her tongue. "So," she said instead, "what will you do? Will you rent another boat and go back to sailing?"

"And dare the devil twice?" He sent her a cautious look that was infuriatingly endearing. "Did I get that right?"

She had to smile. "Yes."

He focused on his handiwork, leaving Summer to study first his dark head, then the thick cords of his neck, then the muscular shelf of his shoulders. "I'm not sure what I'll do," he said quietly, "but whatever it is, I think I'll do it on land."

He didn't look at her, which left her wondering what was going through his mind. There hadn't been anything suggestive in his statement. He sounded as though he meant it when he said that he wasn't sure what he'd do. She imagined him walking into town the next morning, phoning from the grocery store for money and credit cards and taking the noon ferry to the mainland. She imagined him gone and felt a vague sense of disappointment.

He wasn't a bad sort, for a man. He hadn't hurt her when he might have, hadn't criticized the way she lived, hadn't ridiculed her occupation or laughed at her stories of snakes, bugs and puddles in the meadow. He hadn't scoffed at the ponies or her claim that the beech trees were special. He was handsome and undemanding. He could make lunch. And whether at the harpsichord or her knee, he had a way with his hands that was incredible.

The hands in question continued to work, lean, blunt-tipped fingers surrounding her knee, rhythmically pushing, pulling and stroking, seeming to pulse like the sea against the shore. Her whole leg felt relaxed and renewed, and the pleasure was radiating upward. Aware that she was falling into a trap but not caring, she sighed, shuddered, took a deep breath and sighed again. He shot her a quick smile that warmed her, and the warmth lingered, working its way from her eyes to her mouth, then lower, to her breasts and belly. Somewhere along the way it took on a glitter; somewhere it became something that it hadn't been at the start; somewhere it slowed and grew seductive.

Summer caught her breath, but Cameron didn't look up. His hands continued to flex, to knead her knee, but more and more lightly until they were a mere whisper over her skin. Then they separated, one sliding down her shin, the other caressing her thigh. His head remained bent, eyes following the exploration of his hands. She felt her color rise, felt the quickening of her pulse and the stirring of something new.

Then, as though he had all the time in the world, he slowly raised his eyes to hers. *You're lovely,* he said silently. *Soft and feminine. I want to touch more, stroke more, see more.*

*It's a trap,* her tiny voice said but in vain. She caught her breath again as his words slid south from her mind, leaving heat in their wake and an ache that was awesome. She'd never felt an ache like that, deep in the part of her that was uncategorically female. She'd never come close to feeling an ache like that, and though she knew what it was about, she didn't know how to handle it.

*I'm confused,* her eyes cried. *I don't understand what you're doing to me.*

*You understand,* he chided.

But she didn't, because her mother had never told her about feelings like these. Oh, she knew about sex. She knew that men and women turned each other on, and she knew what happened when they did. But that it should happen to her was unthinkable. She had been raised to be independent, to be self-contained and self-sufficient. She had been raised to distrust men. To respond to one this way was frightening.

She was on the verge of telling Cameron that when a loud thudding came at the door. Already in a state of heightened awareness, she gasped.

Cameron put a long finger to her lips, bringing her frightened eyes to his. *It's all right. You're safe. Nothing will ever happen that you don't want. Trust me.*

She took a breath that was rife with the scent of his skin, but rather than arouse her more, it had a blessedly pacifying effect. Her pulse steadied; the ache inside her eased. Only when that had happened did he draw back and stand up. The thudding was coming again, more impatiently this time, when he pulled open the door.

"Yes?" he asked with a gruffness that took Summer by surprise. Loathe to antagonize one of the islanders and bring trouble upon herself, she rose from the chair and went to his side.

Standing just beyond her door was the hulking figure of Morgan Shutter. He wore the yellow oilskins of the fishermen, but beneath his dripping sou'wester, his face was dark and disgruntled.

"Morgan," Summer said politely, "what brings you here in the middle of a storm?"

"My youngest is makin' a godawful noise'n his chest," he said in a voice far gruffer than Cameron's had been. "Ginny says you got to give me somethin' fo'it."

"She doesn't *have* to give you anything," Cameron informed him, drawing himself straighter and, it seemed to Summer, a foot taller than before. But she put a tempering hand on his arm.

"It's all right," she said, then to Morgan, "Is it the croup again?"

"A-yuh."

"Is he feverish?"

He made a disparaging noise and shook his head.

Summer left the door and went into the kitchen, where she began taking various jars and pouches from the shelves.

"Charming man," Cameron remarked when he joined her. "Is he an example of the local color?"

Glad to have something to occupy her, what with her awareness of Cameron lingering in her body, Summer talked as she worked. "He and his brothers and their father are scallopers. They live down by the docks. Morgan and his wife have five children. The oldest is seven."

"Five kids? *That* guy? His wife must be a saint to let him touch her that often. He reeks."

"Shh."

"He does."

Summer wondered whether Cameron was more offended by the smell or by the timing of Morgan's interruption. "That's the fish," she murmured so that Morgan wouldn't hear, though she suspected he was out on the porch. Islanders came to her door when they had to, but they didn't step inside. "Besides, having babies is a way of life here. For people like the Shutters, there isn't much to do at night once the children are asleep."

"They could read."

They could, though as a rule they didn't. And who was Summer to criticize, when she didn't read herself?

"Or watch television like you do," Cameron said.

"Nine chances in ten, their television is broken."

"Why don't they get it fixed?"

"Because the money they'd spend on that is better spent on food for the children. Those children are their future. They're the ones who will grow up to be scallopers and take over the boats when Morgan and his brothers grow old."

"I'm surprised the kids don't grow up and ship out."

"Some do. That's why they need six or seven children."

"You mean, she'll have more?" Cameron asked in dismay.

"Uh-huh. That way they'll be guaranteed at least two or three for the business." She tapped a measure of powder onto a cheesecloth patch. "Are large families so rare where you come from?"

"You bet. Two kids is all we're allowed."

Summer shot him a questioning look. "I didn't know the Canadian government controlled things like that."

He cleared his throat. "What I meant was that limiting families to two children is the in thing. It makes sense, given that the natural resources of any planet are finite."

Summer glanced through the window toward her backyard and the garden that sprawled at its farthermost reaches. In the course of the brief northeast season, that single garden produced enough vegetables to last her the year and then some. "The problem as I see it," she said, cinching the drawstring on one small leather pouch and reaching for another, "is that people don't make the most of their natural resources. Either they're too lazy to make the land work for them, or too greedy, as in logging the forests bare. People on the mainland have mixed-up values. They forget what's important. They make life more complicated than it has to be. Out here, things are simpler."

He was quiet for a moment before saying with curiosity and a bit of confusion, "You sound like you enjoy it."

She looked at him in surprise. "I do. Very much. Did I ever imply that I didn't?"

"No. But here you are with a grumpy oaf standing on your doorstep—"

"Shh!"

"—and chances are he won't even thank you for what you're doing. What are you doing anyway?"

"Mixing something for the baby's croup."

"I see leaves and powders. What happens next?"

"I wrap them in this cheesecloth. When Morgan gets home, he drops the package in boiling water, makes a tent over the pot and holds the baby inside. It works."

He watched her add a few tiny bark chips. "What if it doesn't? I mean, what if the baby is really sick?"

"They'll come back for more tomorrow."

"And if it doesn't work then?"

She closed the last of the pouches and returned them to their shelves. "They'll take him to a hospital on the mainland."

"While they're there, will one of the brothers come and burn your place down?"

She smiled. "No. They'd be afraid to come into my woods on an errand like that. I may not have succeeded in healing the baby, but I've succeeded in enough other cases so that they can't completely rule out my power. *You* may not believe that I have anything to do with what happens in the meadow, but there are plenty of islanders who do. Like I said, there are some who think I'm a witch."

"Do they actually tell you that?"

"Not in as many words." She gathered the corners of the cheesecloth together and wound a piece of thread around the top to keep the ingredients inside. "They sometimes say things that suggest it, but it's okay. Sticks and stones and all. I'm different from them, and therefore threatening."

"But you care for their sick."

"That's my job. It's what I was put here for. I provide a valuable service. Whether they admit it or not doesn't matter. *I* know it. That's all that counts."

"More should count. Have you ever thought of leaving the island?"

"No," she said unequivocably. Taking the cheese-cloth pouch, she went to the front porch and gave it to Morgan. With a grunt, he took it and was gone.

"No pay?" Cameron asked when she closed the door.

"Nope."

"No thanks?"

She held up a hand and said soberly, "Leave it, Cameron. It's my life. If I wanted thanks, I'd be doing something else in some other place." She dropped her hand. "One of the nice things about living alone is that I don't have to answer to anyone. If I don't miss the pay, why should you?" She went to the fireplace to add several logs to the embers. Despite the fact that they had just eaten lunch, the afternoon was wearing on. Before long, it would be night. That thought made her uneasy.

She stared at the fire for a time. The new wood hissed and crackled in a last-ditch protest before submitting to the flames, but submission was inevitable. Split wood was for burning just as healers were for healing. It was fine for Summer to say that if she wanted thanks she'd be doing something else, but the fact was that there was nothing else she could do, nowhere else she could go. This was the only life she had ever known.

"Well?" Cameron asked, propping an elbow on the mantel. "What's the verdict? Do I get dressed and go on into town? Or do I stay here until the rain ends?"

She was torn. Looking at the flames, she tried to imagine herself alone in the cabin, just as she'd always been, but she couldn't seem to erase Cameron's presence from her periphery. He had saved her life; she had thanked him for it. But enough? Could she be so callous as to send him out in the storm? Would one more night really hurt?

"I feel as though you should leave," she said softly. She was falling, falling.

"But you don't want me to."

She tried to rationalize it. "I owe you for saving my life."

"No, you don't. I didn't do anything more than I'd have done anyway for myself. You don't weigh a thing. Carrying you on my back while I swam ashore was no effort. The ocean did the work."

"And carting me all the way up here?"

"Like I said, you don't weigh a thing." His voice deepened. "Besides, I like holding you in my arms."

"That's why you should leave," she blurted.

Hooking a finger under her chin, he tipped up her face, forcing her eyes to his. "Why are you still afraid of me?" he asked.

"Because you're here," she whispered. "And you're different."

"And you want me."

She shook her head in denial, but even as she did, she felt a warmth curling deep inside her. "I don't want any man," she said on the chance that her body would listen. Traitorously, it began a soft trembling.

Cameron took her hands, brought them to his mouth and kissed each palm. Then, while his eyes said, *Don't fight,* he flattened them on his chest.

Summer could barely *breathe,* much less fight. Beneath her fingers, his naked chest was firm and warm and so very alive that she wouldn't have removed her hands for the world. She felt wisps of dark hair swirling beneath her palms, then the buds of his nipples tightening as he inched her hands over him.

He closed his eyes and turned his face aside, looking as though he were in pain.

She tore her hands from his chest and crossed her arms over her own, in part to stem the burning of her breasts as she backed away. "This isn't right. I'm not meant to do it."

"Like hell you aren't," was Cameron's hoarse response, but he had turned toward the mantel and was bracing his forehead on an arm there. The pose put a bend in his body. Summer dared look at the front of his jeans and knew from the distension there that the pose was deliberate.

He wanted her. No man had ever wanted her before. The one who had dragged her into the woods and torn at her clothes had had a violation in mind. He hadn't wanted her in the sense of feeling desire. But Cameron did.

Was that what her father had felt for her mother? Or her grandfather for her grandmother? Had those women felt the same ache she did? Had they trembled, too?

"You have to leave," she whispered, pressing her fingertips to her lips. "I don't want to want anyone."

Cameron gave a harsh chuckle. "And you think I do? This wasn't supposed to happen." Taking an uneven breath, he forced himself to straighten. "Wasn't supposed to happen," he muttered, flexing his shoulders.

The movement caught Summer's eye. She curled her hands into fists by way of fighting the urge to touch him.

Without looking at her, he went to the harpsichord and, setting a knee on the bench, picked out a one-handed tune. It was new to Summer this time, was faster, hotter, more impassioned than before. It spoke of the inner turmoil that she was feeling herself, and wasn't quick to be calmed. Rather, as though one hand alone simply couldn't exorcise the frustration, his other hand joined the fray.

Summer sank into a corner of the sofa, pressed her cheek to its arm and squeezed her eyes shut, but no amount of compression could distort the images she saw there. They were beautiful images, highly erotic ones, and hot, so very hot that she began to breathe more quickly. She saw Cameron's hands on her body, saw that her body was bare. She saw them circle her ribs and move to her breasts. Feeling took over then—the kneading of swelling flesh, the near-painful hardening of her nipples between his fingers. She felt a pull between her legs seconds before his hands went there, and then, quite helplessly, she was opening to him, letting him do to her anything and everything he could, and the feeling was so new, the pleasure so intense that she could only catch in a high, mewling sound and go with the pulsing rhythm of orgasm.

# 4

WHEN SUMMER AWOKE the next morning, she was in her bed in the loft, with the pale glow on the rafters telling her the sun was up. She couldn't remember much of the night before beyond bits of music, and at first assumed that she'd spent the evening listening to the stereo. Then she remembered Cameron and sat bolt upright in bed.

He wasn't in the loft, as he'd been the morning before, but she had only to lean off the bed for a view of the cabin below to see him sprawled face down on the sofa. One leg hung over the end, the other over the side. Both were bare beneath the towel that circled his hips.

She sat straight up again. Something had happened. She remembered feeling warm. She remembered feeling aroused. Even now there was a new sensitivity inside. But when she tried to bring back details, nothing came. It was like she'd been drugged again. The hours were a blank.

Silently she climbed from bed, crept down the stairs and tiptoed to where Cameron lay. He hadn't moved. His back was smooth and symmetrical, the skin drawn taut on either side of his spine by his arms, which were flung out at shoulder level. She tiptoed farther so that she could see his face. Even in repose it was bold. But he had shaved, she realized, and his hair looked clean. He must have taken a shower, which explained the towel around his hips, which made her feel better, but only to a point. If something had happened *before* he'd taken that shower, she was in trouble. If she had sampled something that would make her want him again and again, she could kiss her future peace of mind goodbye.

She feared something had. What else explained the new awareness she felt or the continuing urge she had to touch him?

In self-defense, she escaped into the bathroom. A long shower helped, as did the knowledge that normalcy had returned in the form of electricity. Mostly, though, what helped was the knowledge that the sun was out, that the storm was over, that Cameron would leave and life would be the way it was.

He had to leave whether she liked it or not, she told the image in the mirror, whose long blond hair was a flaxen shawl on her shoulders and whose cheeks were unusually pink. Life had to return to normal.

A light knock came at the door. "Summer? Are you okay?"

"Sure," she called out. "I'm just about done. Be right there."

She hurried, knowing that the sooner he was gone, the better. But the instant she opened the door, she felt the catch in her heart that was becoming all too familiar. Cameron was sitting on the sofa with his head back and his eyes closed. He had put on his jeans, but the snap was undone, and she couldn't blame him for that. The jeans were corrugated with dried wrinkles. They looked dreadfully uncomfortable.

He opened his eyes, which looked nearly as uncomfortable as the jeans. "How'd you sleep?"

"Like a log."

He nodded, then sat forward, propping his elbows on his knees. "About last night . . ."

"What about it?" Determined to play it cool, she kept a firm grip on the thudding of her heart.

He regard her cautiously. "Do you remember much?"

"I remember your playing the harpsichord," she said and could have sworn she saw a look of guilt touch his face. "I must have fallen asleep after that. Did something happen?"

"No. I just played, but I got a little carried away. By the time I was done, you were out of it again. I tried to get you up for dinner, but you said you wanted to sleep. I figured you were still working the trauma of being shipwrecked out of your system."

"That must have been it." She prayed it was true, but she hadn't liked that look of guilt. Something had happened. She knew it had. But she couldn't say exactly what it was, and she was too embarrassed to prod Cameron, so she played dumb.

Gathering her hair at the nape of her neck, she secured it with a ribbon and forced out a nonchalant, "I'm really hungry. I could go for eggs, bacon and home fries, but I don't have any of those here. Why don't we go into town? You can make your phone calls, then I'll treat you to breakfast before you leave."

He frowned. "You don't have to treat me."

"You saved my life. Of course I have to treat you. Besides, you have no money, remember?"

"One phone call, and I'll have my credit card number. I can charge breakfast."

"Not on the Isle of Pride you can't. It's cash or nothing here."

Cameron's frown grew perplexed. "You got nothing last night from Morgan Shutter. So where do you get the cash?"

He kept returning to that. She wasn't sure why he did, but since he'd be out of her life before the day was done, she didn't see the harm in telling the truth. It was no big thing. "When my mother died, I inherited some money. It earns interest. I live on that."

He was as perplexed as ever. "But your mother was a healer, too. Where did *she* get the money?"

"From my grandmother."

"Who was a healer, too. Are you sure there wasn't a significant male somewhere along the line?"

"No, there was not a significant male," Summer replied, vaguely annoyed that that would be Cameron's solution. Her ancestors had been liberated women long before liberation became the thing. They'd had to be liberated. The men in their lives had been good for one thing, and it wasn't money. "Somewhere back in the time of my great-great-grandmother, a small nest egg was set aside. It's grown. I never spend as much interest as there is, so the principal compounds."

"I see," he said, though he didn't sound convinced. Summer didn't know why. It sounded perfectly logical to her.

But there was no point dwelling on the matter. Whether Cameron believed her was irrelevant, since he would be gone within hours.

Her heart caught. She ignored it.

"I'm going into town," she said. "Are you coming?"

THE WALK INTO TOWN took fifteen minutes, each step of which was a tonic to Summer. The sun was warm and regenerative, the air laden with the scent of the rich, wet earth. Her knee worked like a dream, belying its injury less than two days before. It carried her at a brisk pace that Cameron matched with ease.

"If I weren't here," he asked, "what would you be doing today?"

"The same thing I am now. I've been gone for two weeks. I have to pick up the mail and buy some food."

"So you'd carry all that home, and then what?"

"Then I'd go to the meadow and play with the ponies, maybe clean up some of the branches that were blown down in the woods."

"Then what?"

"Then I'd work in the garden. If I don't put up those vegetables soon, the ripe ones will spoil."

"Then what?"

"Then I don't know. Whatever I feel like doing."

He pondered that, finally saying, "Not bad."

"That's what I've been telling you. My life may be different from yours or someone else's, but I like it just fine." She repeated the last phrase silently, once, then a second time, and would have gone for a third and made it a mantra if she'd felt it necessary. She didn't think it was. Summer VanVorn didn't do foolish things like fall for smooth talk, a virile body and navy blue eyes. She went her own way, keeping her independence intact.

They walked on in silence. In time, they passed small wood frame houses, one by one. With each successive block, the one by ones came closer together until the center of town was at hand.

"Is this it?" Cameron asked, looking dubiously around.

"Uh-huh. General store, post office, luncheonette and inn."

"How many rooms at the inn?"

"Four. We don't cater to tourists." She pointed down the street. "The dock is three blocks that way. The streets surrounding it are lined with the fishermen's homes. The bait houses and fuel pumps are right by the pier." She turned toward the post office, which was housed in a small, weathered shed. "I'm stopping here first. Why don't you go on to the store. There's a phone you'll be able to use. I'll meet you there when I'm done."

Hoping that her dismissal was firm enough, she strode to the door of the post office, daring to look back only when she was inside. She was relieved to see Cameron disappear into the store.

With a tiny sigh, she turned to the woman who sat behind the window engrossed in a dog-eared paperback novel. Millie Osgood was the postmistress for the Isle of Pride. An octogenarian with a halo of blue curls circling her head, she was arthritic and slightly hard of hearing. She was also the only person on Pride who came close to being a friend to Summer.

"Millie?" Summer called, then more loudly, *"Millie?"*

Millie looked up. For a minute, she seemed disoriented, as though she was still in the world of her book and couldn't grasp the fact of Summer's interruption. With dawning recognition, her wrinkled face broke into a smile.

"Why, hello, Summer." Flattening the novel onto her desk, she braced her weight on it and with some effort pushed herself up. "Back from your travels, are you?"

"I am," Summer said with a nod to reinforce the words.

"You missed quite a storm. Not yet the one your mama was predicting, but it blew around real good."

"I know. I lost my boat."

*"Did* you now?"

Summer nodded. She liked Millie, as had her mother, because Millie wasn't judgmental the way the rest of the town was. Granted, if someone else walked into the post office while Summer was there, Millie would give that person her attention. But when she turned back, there was always a smile, usually even an apology, something no one else in town would dream of giving. That apology would have endeared Millie to Summer, even if Millie weren't a help in other ways as well.

"You don't look to be hurt," the postmistress said, squinting at Summer. "Color's a little high, mebbe, but other'n that, you look fine."

"I am fine," Summer assured her in a loud voice. "How are *you*? You must have felt the rain in your bones." Taking a muslin pouch from the large canvas bag that hung from her shoulder, she passed it over the counter. "Tea. In case you're low."

"Why, thank you," the old woman said, tucking the pouch into the pocket of her skirt. "You're good to remember me. Your mama always did, too. Can't buy this tea in any store, y'know." She turned to the wall of narrow cubbies and pulled an armful of mail from one. "Here we go." Setting the mail on the counter, she began to sort through. "Advertisement, advertisement, advertisement," she sang, laying aside the first three. "You don't want leather jackets, film processing or encyclopedias, do you?"

Summer smiled and shook her head.

Millie held up the next two envelopes. "Bills."

Summer took them. She frowned at what was next in the pile. "More catalogues? They keep sending them, even though I never buy a thing. I don't understand how they get my name."

"Come again?" Millie said, cupping her ear.

"How do they get my name?" Summer asked more loudly.

Millie passed across a package. "From this."

Recognizing the logo in the corner, Summer's eyes lit up. She quickly opened the padded bag. Inside were audiocassettes. As each emerged, Millie read its label.

"You have here *A Brief History of Time, The Civil War, Jurassic Park, Buffalo Girls* and *Dazzle*. That what you ordered?"

Nodding, Summer reached for another package. "And the videos." She tore at the box.

"There's *Dances With Wolves,*" Millie read, "*Great American Cities, Ghost* and *Around the World in 80 Days.* That right?"

"That's right," Summer said, feeling the same sense of anticipation she always felt when her orders arrived. Properly rationed, they would provide entertainment for the month.

"I'm afraid this is for you, too," Millie said, apologetic now. She showed Summer a letter that had no stamp or postmark, simply Summer's name on the front. "Shall I read it for you?"

"Please." It would be a message from the selectmen who governed the Isle of Pride. Summer guessed what the message would concern.

Millie pushed her spectacles higher on her nose. "Miss VanVorn," she read and cleared her throat. "This to officially tell you that the OSAY Company will be here on the Isle of Pride on the twenty-eighth of August to look into building a satellite tracking station in the meadow near your land. Such a station would bring money to the local citizenry without disrupting the island life. We don't want trouble when the OSAY people come. So if you have any objection to the project, you better tell us beforehand. If you want a meeting, make an appointment. Also, we voted that you should stay home on your own land while the company people is here."

Summer gave a grim sigh. "A satellite tracking station. What will they think of next?"

Millie snorted. "Why they tell you beforehand is beyond me. If you didn't know they were comin', you couldn't do nothing to the meadow."

"It's not me that does things," Summer scolded. "I don't have that kind of power."

"Tell that to the selectmen."

"I have. They don't believe me." Taking the letter from Millie, she folded it and put it in the canvas bag with the rest of her mail. "The twenty-eighth," she mused. "That's five days from now."

"Come again?"

But Summer shook her head. She would have to meet with the selectmen, who would do their best to convince her that the project was in the best interests of the islanders. She would argue on behalf of the ponies of Pride, but, if experience held, her arguments would be for naught. The selectmen would show the corporation around the meadow, while Summer prayed for something distasteful to happen.

None of that had to trouble Millie, though, and Summer had other stops to make. So she thanked the postmistress with a warm smile, left the post office and crossed the street to the general store. She was nearly there when the Mundy brothers came out the door. They were in their late teens, with cases of acne that Summer would have been happy to cure if they'd been kinder, but they had smart mouths and an air of invincibility that allowed them to use those mouths without restraint.

"Lookee here," said the mean one, Sam. "If it ain't the rain lady. That was some storm you brewed up. Who you tryin' to drown this time? Ain't no one comin' to the meadow this week."

"She's slippin'," said the ugly one, George. "Must be that time of the month."

Sam snickered. "Witches don't bleed like normal women. They *ain't* normal women. Their insides is made o' straw."

"Got straw inside?" George asked Summer. "Got straw with little bugs running up and down and around?"

"Excuse me," Summer said quietly. Given her druthers, she'd have gone out of her way to avoid the brothers. They were taller than she and troublesome even to the other islanders. But there was only one way into the general store, so she walked between them.

"Waste of blond hair," Sam jeered.

"Any bugs up there?" George asked.

"Any problem?" came a different voice. Summer raised her eyes to Cameron's as he opened the door for her.

"No," she said softly. "They're leaving."

Cameron eyed the brothers with something less than affection as he asked her, "What did they say?"

"Nothing."

"That so?" he asked them, arching a brow.

"I said somethin'," Sam declared, but before he had a chance to repeat it, he started to cough.

Cameron looked at George. "Do you care to add to that?"

"Who're you?" George demanded while his brother coughed.

"Someone who has more respect for a lady than you apparently do."

"She's no la—" His voice broke before the word was out. Putting a hand to his throat, he tried to clear it. He coughed and tried again, coughed and tried again.

"Must be the dust," Cameron told Summer, who, with great curiosity, watched the boys stumble off.

"Did you do that?" she whispered because there was no dust, not on the heels of the rain they'd had.

"Me?" he whispered back. "I thought *you* did it."

"No. I was wishing the hiccups on them. But wishing's about all I can do. I don't have the power to make things happen." She figured there was a cold going through the Mundy family. That would explain the boys' coughs.

"Hiccups." Cameron smiled. "Not bad."

Summer looked at him, then looked again. He was wearing a new pair of jeans, a new jersey and a pair of new boat shoes. "Not bad, yourself," she said. He looked spectacular. "I take it you had no trouble getting a cash advance on your credit card."

"Nope."

A gravelly voice came from just inside the door. "Is she bothering you, young man?"

Glancing into the shadows from the brilliantly sunny street, Summer could make out Ezra Whittle, the owner of the general store. Ezra was the antithesis of Millie. He had never had much patience for the VanVorns.

"Bothering me?" Cameron asked. "Of course not. Why would she be bothering me?"

"She's the local medicine lady is why," Ezra said. "Medicine ladies is always strange."

"Actually," Cameron replied, "I thought those two boys who just left here were more strange than she is, and she's a damn sight prettier." To Summer, in a voice that Ezra could easily hear, he said, "Can your shopping wait a bit? I need some air. It's too stuffy for comfort in that old store." Taking her arm, he steered her down the street toward the luncheonette.

Summer had never had a champion before and didn't know what to make of it. Customarily, she simply abided the rude comments while she gathered what she needed in town and left. Having someone take her side was a novel experience—pleasant, actually. She knew that the eyes of the town were on Cameron and her as they walked down the street. To be seen with someone as impressive would set the natives to talking for weeks.

That was fine for her, not so fine for Cameron. "It's a good thing you're leaving," she advised. "You won't win any friends here by keeping company with me."

"I haven't met anyone yet I'd care to have as a friend, except you," he replied crossly. "What's the trouble with these people? How can they be so callous? Don't they think about other people's feelings?"

"As far as they're concerned, I don't have feelings. I'm a witch. I'm not normal."

"Like hell you're not," he gritted out, "and why are you taking *their* side?"

"I'm not taking their side. I'm simply explaining why they are the way they are. It's always been this way. Nothing I do or say will change it, so why should I make the effort? I'm polite, I pay for whatever I buy at the time of purchase, I heal if I'm called to heal. I give the people here every reason to think the best of me. If they choose not to, my confronting them won't help. Besides," she added, taking a grimmer tone, "I'll have to confront them about the meadow again. I just got a notice that there's another group coming to visit."

"Another?"

"A company looking to put up a satellite tracking station."

"Interesting."

"It's not! It's horrible!"

"Of course it is, from your perspective. But you have to admit that a satellite tracking station is more constructive than a resort or a golf course."

"But I don't want *anything* in the meadow," she cried. "I thought you understood that!"

"I do," he said, then repeated it more quietly as he guided her into the luncheonette.

Summer, too, grew quiet. She was acutely aware that the dozen or so patrons of the restaurant had stopped talking the instant she and Cameron had entered. All eyes were on them. She led the way to the booth farthest from the counter where most of those patrons were sitting, and slid in. Cameron did the same. She handed him a menu from behind the napkin dispenser.

"The omelets are good," she told him in a low voice. "So's the French toast. And the home fries."

Without a glance at the menu, Cameron said, "They're staring. Do I look funny, or are they just surprised to see us together?"

"They're surprised. I don't come in here often, and when I do, I sit alone."

"Y'know, Summer, I don't understand that. Fine, you're a healer, so they're wary of you. But you look perfectly normal, and you *act* perfectly normal, and I'd guess you're probably ten times prettier than any of those guys' wives." He scowled at the man at the end of the counter nearest them. "I can understand why *that* guy doesn't come close. He knows you'd never be attracted to anyone so slovenly." Turning to her, he asked, "How many of these people would you say you've treated over the years?"

"I've treated someone in the family of most every one."

"And still they behave this way?" He looked at the slovenly one, Jeb Strunk. "What's his problem?"

"Leave it, Cameron. It's okay."

"It's not," Cameron snapped, but he did turn to Summer. "What he's doing is rude. It would serve him right if—"

He was interrupted by a loud crack that was followed by a thunderous roll. Summer's eyes shot to the floor by the counter, where Jeb Strunk was sprawled after toppling from his broken stool. She stared in helpless fascination, then blinked and forced her eyes to Cameron's.

"You *did* that," she whispered, moving her lips as little as possible, though with Jeb's fall the attention had left them.

"Me?" he whispered. "He did it himself. I'm amazed the stool held him as long as it did. He needs to go on a diet. Doesn't he know that being overweight causes things like heart disease, high blood pressure and cancer?"

Obesity and its consequences were the last things on Summer's mind. "How did you do it?" she asked in awe. She guessed that if he was a magician, sleight of hand had been involved, but she hadn't seen him touch anything near where Jeb had been sitting. "Maybe telekinesis?" She had heard about that. If Cameron was gifted that way, he might have used the power of his mind to bend the metal under the seat of Jeb's stool. "It had to be that. Nothing else could have snapped the seat off that way."

"His weight did it," Cameron muttered and looked at the approaching waitress. "Know what you want?" he asked Summer.

"Yes." To the waitress, who kept glancing nervously at where Jeb was hauling himself off the floor, she said, "I'll have a cheese omelet with bacon and biscuits, home fries and a large cranberry juice."

"Ditto for me," Cameron said.

The woman wrote down the order and ran off. "See now," Summer chided, "you've terrified her. If she thinks I'm a witch, she's assuming you're a warlock. She'll have nightmares for days."

"Good," Cameron declared darkly. "If it takes a convenient coincidence to teach her a lesson in respect, so by it."

"Be it. So be it."

"Yeah, well, you get my draft."

"Drift. Not draft."

"Sorry. My mind doesn't work right when I get annoyed."

Summer had the same problem, which was one of the reasons she didn't let herself get annoyed. Inevitably, though, it happened from time to time, so she knew what to do. "Take a deep breath," she told Cameron, who looked skeptical. "Go on. Take a deep breath. Fill your lungs as full as you can. That's right. Now slowly, slowly release the breath, and while you do, make a deliberate attempt to relax. Concentrate on letting go of that irritation. Think soothing thoughts." She paused. "Better?"

He let go of the last of that deep breath and took a more normal one. "Yeah. What was that?"

"The simplest form of mind control, though my talking *you* through it is absurd, given what you just did."

He rolled his eyes and said in a facetious way, "Ah, yes, the bar stool. Wait till you see some of the *other* things I have up my sleeve."

But there wouldn't be time for that, Summer realized, feeling a pang. "Did you buy a ticket for the ferry?"

"Not yet."

"Maybe you should run back and tell Ezra you want one."

"What's the rush?"

"The ferry isn't always punctual. On a calm day like this, it may pull up to the dock at eleven-thirty. It'll leave if it doesn't know to wait for a passenger."

Cameron glanced at the wall clock. "It's barely nine. There's plenty of time." He rested his elbows on the table. "Tell me more about the satellite tracking station."

Summer pulled out the letter and slid it across the table. While he read it, her eyes drifted helplessly over his jersey. For a minute she wondered what it would be like if she were like other women. She wondered what it would be like to follow arousal through to its end. With a man like Cameron, she guessed it would be heavenly.

"Do they always send you letters like this?" he asked.

She nodded, struggling to focus.

"Do you meet with them?"

She swallowed. "For what it's worth. We've never been able to resolve our differences. So far, I've been lucky. Something always puts off the buyer. One of these times, I won't be so lucky."

He set the letter down and looked her straight in the eye. "Tell me the truth. Those things that happen, do you cause them?"

She shook her head. "My mother might have, but with each generation, the power is weakened. Mine isn't strong at all."

"Then what explains the goings-on in the meadow?"

"What explained the parting of the Red Sea?"

"I don't know. I wasn't on earth back then."

"It was a fluke of nature. The Red Sea, my snakes, puddles and bugs—all flukes of nature."

"True believers would disagree. They'd call you blasphemous."

"They're already thinking it, so what's the harm?" She sighed. "Believe me, I wish it weren't so. I wish I could take credit for what happens in the meadow, because then I could go off and plan something new to happen this time."

"Like what?" he asked. "If you did have the power to make things happen, what would you wish for?"

A slow smile came to her lips. "I don't know. Let me think." While she was doing that, the waitress delivered breakfast. Summer began to eat, thinking all the while. Finally, with a wicked gleam in her eye, she said, "Cow dung."

Cameron choked on his biscuit. He took a quick gulp of juice and thumped his chest several times. "Cow dung?"

"Cow dung."

"You're bad."

But she didn't care, since she was only imagining. "I can just see it. There they'd go, the selectmen in their plaid pants that are inches too short and their polyester blazers, and the company men in their natty Harris tweed suits, walking confidently across the meadow, and then, *splat*, someone would step right into a huge, thick, wet cow pie, and then someone else would step in another, and another, and another. They'd just pop up out of nowhere. And then, just in case anyone thought my ponies were doing the harm, there'd be pies popping up all the way into town. Those men with their once-shiny wing-tipped shoes would want to get off the island as soon as possible and never come back."

"You're *bad*," Cameron repeated, but he was grinning. "And how'd a country girl like you learn about natty business suits and wing-tipped shoes?"

"They're always mentioned in books. Haven't you read *Bonfire of the Vanities?*"

"No," he said after a moment's consideration, "I'm afraid I haven't."

"Then you can watch the movie," she suggested. "I have it back at the . . . cabin." Her words slowed. "But you'll be gone," she said with less enthusiasm. "Try to catch it when you go home." She turned her attention to her breakfast, which was nowhere near as tasty as it had been moments before.

They ate in silence for a time, during which the waitress dashed up, delivered two coffees and a handful of creams and dashed off. The counter had cleared since they'd arrived. People were going off to see to business. Time was passing.

Cameron cleared his throat. "I've been thinking."

He did that a lot. It made him even more appealing to Summer, who was used to the shoot-from-the-hip bluntness of the islanders.

"I could stay on a few days, if you wanted. I'm not in any rush to get back home."

Summer's heart had started to skitter. "You can't stay here," she said automatically.

"I wouldn't stay at your cabin, of course. I'd stay at the inn."

She shook her head. "They wouldn't give you a room. Not now."

"Why not?"

"You've been seen with me," she explained, feeling and regretting each word. If only she were like other women. If only. "The Mundys will be spreading stories. So will Ezra. So will Jeb, for that matter, and everyone else who saw what happened here."

"But I just spent a bundle in Ezra's store."

"Doesn't matter. You branded yourself when you stuck up for me."

"Then the damage is already done, so there'll be no harm if I stay longer."

"There'll be harm," Summer said. Her eyes found his and didn't budge. "Living alone is all I've known for the past ten years. I'm used to it. If you stay longer, I'm apt to get used to having you around. I can't let that happen."

He held out a hand in a no-big-deal gesture. "One week. That's all. I can help you do the things you shouldn't do until your knee is back to normal."

"It's already back to normal."

He arched a brow. "Can you honestly say that you don't feel a throbbing there sometimes?"

Now that he mentioned it, she did feel a throbbing. It hadn't been there moments before. Maybe she just hadn't been *thinking* of it moments before. "I can manage."

"Come on, Summer. I got a look at that garden of yours. It's huge. You say you want to can vegetables so that you'll have them for winter. Why not let me help? You'll finish in half the time with the knee even better than it is now."

The knee was throbbing. She didn't understand. It had felt so good until then.

Rubbing it with one hand, she said, "I can put up the vegetables myself," but she was sorely tempted to accept his offer. If, indeed, her knee was reacting negatively to the walk into town, it didn't bode well for the ups and downs of work in the garden.

At least, that was one excuse for letting him stay.

"And then there's the matter of the selectmen," Cameron said, giving her another. "Could be that a man standing up with you at that meeting would have more effect than your standing there alone."

Summer doubted that. Her meetings with the selectmen were a mere formality. The three men listened to her arguments, made their counterarguments, then smiled and stood and said how pleased they were that things had been settled. They never truly heard her. They never believed that the ponies of Pride were unique.

"Let me stay," Cameron coaxed. "If not at the inn, then on the sofa in the cabin. I can make things easier for you." His voice grew deeper. "I'd like to do that. I'd like it a lot. But mostly, I'd like you to trust me."

*Trust me. Trust me.* Over and over he'd said it, yet it was the one thing Summer found hardest of all. Compounding the dilemma now was the issue of whether she could trust herself. If she fell for Cameron, if she let him stay, if something happened between them and then he left, she'd be crushed.

Her mother had been crushed when her father had left. He had come off the ferry, a stranger on the island for one night, and she'd fallen in love with him. Summer had been a product of that love, which was all well and good, except that Summer remembered the horribly helpless feeling she'd had each time her mother took out his farewell note and cried.

But her father had only stayed for a night. Likewise, her grandfather, great-grandfather and great-great-grandfather. Perhaps this was different. "One week?" she asked hesitantly.

"Give or take," he answered. "I'll certainly stay until the harvest is done. Longer if you're comfortable with it. I'm in no immediate rush."

*Tell him no!* the tiny voice inside her demanded. *Make him leave! You're asking for trouble, Summer, big trouble!*

Eyes down, she said, "If something happens and I change my mind, if I need to be alone, if I ask you to leave, will you?"

"Not without trying to convince you otherwise."

She leveled him a gaze. "Will you leave if I ask it?"

His eyes held hers, silently at first, then projecting a message that was melodic and pure and, in that, more effective than any words could have been. He would leave if she wished, it told her.

Summer could only hope that she would be able to wish it when the time inevitably came for it to be so.

# 5

WEDNESDAY WAS FOR GREEN beans. Cameron picked them and brought them inside in batches, while Summer packed them into mason jars, covered them with boiling water and processed them in her pressure canner. She waited for him to make a misstep and give her an excuse to ask him to leave, but he was a model of obedience. She showed him how to snap beans from the vine, and he did it. She showed him how to trim their ends, and he did that, too. She didn't even have to repeat herself; he caught on the first time. More than once she turned to do something, only to find it already done. He was a tremendous help in that sense.

In another sense, he was no help at all. By midday he had taken off his shirt, and could she criticize him? He was warm working in the sun. Sweat trickled from his hairline down his cheeks; his chest and back were glossy with it. And she was tormented. Her body hummed when he came close; it tingled even when he didn't. She told herself not to look at him, but her eyes betrayed the command. She told herself not to go *near* him, but her legs disobeyed. She tried not to touch him, and she didn't, but her hands grew tense with restraint.

Come nightfall, the law of relativity kicked in. She wouldn't touch Cameron, she certainly wouldn't let him touch her, and under *no* conditions would she let him sleep in her bed. But compared to those things, sharing thoughts and feelings with him seemed harmless enough.

They were relaxing on the front porch, drinking iced tea beneath a quarter moon, when he asked, "What do you want from life, Summer? I mean, in the long run, what are your goals?"

She pondered the question, trying to pin down those goals, but they wouldn't stay still. "There is no long run," she said at last. "Not in the sense of years and years. Things happen, unpredictable things sometimes, and goals change. A goal that makes total sense today might be absolutely absurd tomorrow, depending on what happens between now and then." She smiled. "At least, that was what my mother always said. She was convinced that a big storm was coming. I mean a *big* storm that would wipe out the island as we know it."

"Do you believe one will?"

"No. There's nothing in history to support anything as cataclysmic as that. Even if global warming occurs, the rise of the seas will be gradual."

"You know about that?"

"About global warming? Sure. Who doesn't?"

"Plenty of people." He found her eyes in the dark. The moon was too dim to illuminate them, but she felt his curiosity. "You're remarkable. Here you are on a secluded island, yet you're knowledgeable on nearly every subject, and without benefit of newspapers or magazines."

"I have television and radio," she pointed out. "Between the two, I get more current news than I would from any newspaper or magazine."

"You don't read books, either." He had learned that on the way back from town, when she'd told him about the audiocassettes she'd received.

"I listen to them," she reminded him.

"But they're abridged."

"Only a few." Given the choice, she ordered the unabridged versions, since she had all the time in the world to listen. Only two of the five she'd just received were abridged. Of course, they were the ones Cameron had seen.

"But don't you miss something in the translation? When a book is abridged for taping, you only get part of the story."

"Usually it's the best part. Most books are longer than they need to be. You've seen some of the books inside. They're *volumes*."

"They're also ancient," he observed. "Were they your mother's?"

"Mostly. Books on tape didn't become readily available until after she died."

In the night's stillness, a cricket began to chirp.

"Tell me about her, Summer. How did she die?"

Summer sipped her tea. "She got sick."

"Sick how?"

"I don't know. Just sick."

"What was wrong?"

She turned the glass in quick little twists on her thigh. Her mother's death wasn't something she usually thought about, because even after ten years it frustrated her. "She couldn't eat. She started sleeping most of the time. It was like her energy just left her."

"Did she fight it?"

"I guess she did."

"What do you mean, you guess?"

Reluctantly Summer recalled those awful days. "She didn't specifically say that she was fighting it, but I can't imagine she'd willingly go off and leave me that way."

"Did you try to treat her?"

"Of course. I tried everything I knew. When nothing helped, I suggested we see a doctor on the mainland, but she refused. So I tried new things. Nothing worked. She just got weaker and weaker, and then one morning she didn't wake up."

After a short silence, he said, "I'm sorry."

"No sorrier than I am," Summer heard herself say. And then, as though he'd opened a Pandora's box, she cried, "It just didn't make sense. She was always in good health. She never had a cold, never had a virus, never even a toothache, and if she'd only had any of those things, she'd have known how to treat them. She was a healer. It was her life's trade. But in the end she couldn't heal herself. And I wasn't good enough to do the healing for her."

"You blame yourself?" he asked in disbelief.

"Of course I blame myself. She taught me the craft, but I couldn't use it."

"She couldn't, either, so why are you to blame any more than she was? Maybe what killed her was something that was beyond treating with natural medicines. Sounds to me like she might have made a conscious decision to die."

Summer had often thought that, too. "She kept telling me it was time, but that made no sense. She was in her forties. Too young to die." She jiggled the ice in her glass and looked into the darkness of the forest.

From the stillness on the porch came Cameron's deep voice. "Do you believe in life after death?"

Summer wanted to. Death frightened her. Regardless of how odd people thought her, she was conventional in that sense. "I don't know."

"Did your mother?"

"Yes. There were times when she seemed almost eager to die." Summer's voice dropped to a shade above a whisper. "That hurt the most."

"You thought she was eager to leave you? No, Summer. That wasn't it."

"How do you know?"

"I just do. Sometimes when people know that the end of one form of existence is at hand, the only way they can handle it is to look forward to the next."

"Then you believe in life after death?"

"You bet. Only I don't define death as you do. I see it as a change in form. That's all."

She was intrigued. "A change in form?"

"From physical to nonphysical. What is it they say, the spirit loves on—"

"Lives on."

"—lives on in those left behind?"

"That's not really life after death," she chided. "It's just one person having an effect on another that lasts after the first person dies. When the second person dies, the first person is gone completely."

"No, no. What the second person has of the first lives on in a third."

"Not recognizably."

"Does that matter? Come on, Summer, for a witch you're pretty cynical. But okay, another change of form occurs with reincarnation."

"You believe in *that?*" Summer asked in surprise. She had seen movies about reincarnation, but had never taken it seriously.

"I think it happens in some instances," he affirmed, "just like in some instances an earthly body becomes otherworldly."

"Otherworldly," she mused. She remembered when she had wondered if Cameron was that. "Explain."

He set down his glass. "I don't know if I should. You'll think I'm crazy."

"No one's crazier than I am. Go ahead."

Taking a breath, he said, "Okay. Earth is part of the solar system, correct?"

"Correct."

"And the solar system is part of the Milky Way, correct?"

"Correct."

"And the Milky Way is one of millions of galaxies that makes up the universe, correct?"

"That's what scientists say. I've never been out there myself."

"Most humans haven't, but I say that there are life forms in some of those other galaxies, and that some of those life forms are so much more advanced than Earth life forms that they've been coming and going around here for eons."

"Martians in our midst?" Summer asked with a grin, because what he was saying was entertaining.

"Not Martians with crinkly red skin and bug eyes and antennae sticking out of their heads. But human beings who harbor the souls of aliens. When their human shells age and die, they're reclaimed by the home life form."

"Is the human shell aware of having an alien soul?" she asked, still amused.

"Not usually. But once the reclaiming's been done, the alien is aware of having lived as a human."

"But it's not life after death if the human dies."

"Sure it is, if the human was alien all along."

"Then the alien lives on, so there was never a death." Summer pushed herself to her feet. "You're talking semantics, Cameron. Now, if you were to tell me that there's an alien presence on earth that swoops down when a person dies and flies off with the body to a distant planet where the person comes back to life in an alien form, *that'd* be life after death."

He rose beside her. "I could arrange it."

"You could, hmm?" Grinning still, she took the glass from his hand and started into the house. "Know something? I think you're as crazy as I am."

THURSDAY WAS FOR PEAS. Summer showed Cameron how to pick them and shell them, then she took off for the meadow to be alone with the ponies. Convinced that he had enough to occupy him for hours, she took her pipe from the stump of the pine and began to play. She wasn't surprised by what the music said.

She liked Cameron, liked him a lot. She had really enjoyed talking with him on the porch the night before. Not that she bought his theories of life after death, but he presented them with such earnestness that she had to respect him. But respect was only one of the things she felt for him.

Putting the pipe down with a sigh, she thought about that. He was easy to be with, easy to look at, easy to talk with. She had the awful feeling that she was falling in love with him, which was tragic. Because love had nowhere to go. Cameron couldn't stay on Pride and she couldn't leave. History was repeating itself, and the worst of it was that she couldn't fight it. Try as she might to tell herself to send him away before the damage was irreparable, she couldn't. Rather, she found herself slipping the pipe into its sheath, bidding the ponies goodbye and returning to the cabin, where he was.

WHEN THE PEAS had been packed and processed, cooled and labeled, Cameron asked her to show him around the island. She agreed readily, and it wasn't only that her knee was fine and she wanted the exercise. There were parts of the Isle of Pride that she loved, beyond her cabin and the meadow. She wanted Cameron to see those places before he left.

So they walked down the road and over the heath to the boulders facing the mainland. Set in a semicircular pattern, they were like a natural amphitheater. Summer took a seat at the top. Motioning Cameron beside her, she pointed out the nearby islands, then, in the far, far distance and visible only because the day was clear, the mainland.

He sat close, with an arm braced behind her. "Ever been to Bangor?"

She remembered that first day—hard to believe it was only four days before—when he'd carried her from the sea and set her beneath an outcropping of rocks. She'd had the same sheltered feeling then that she did now, and she'd been dazed and hurting then. Now she was aware only of pleasure. "Uh-huh. The lab where I took the beech leaves is in Bangor."

"Ever been to Portland?"

"No."

"Boston?"

"Uh-uh."

"New York?"

She shook her head. "I could never survive in cities like those."

"Not even for a visit?"

Looking over the water in a southerly direction where those cities would lie, she considered it. After several minutes, she shook her head again. "They'd be too strange. Too busy. Too confusing. I'd be too nervous."

"But you have videotapes of all those places."

"Because they fascinate me—the cars, the lights, the people. Whenever I get the urge to see them, I watch the videos. It satisfies the urge." She looked up. His face was inches above hers, his eyes deep and rich, his skin warm, his lips leanly masculine and tempting. "Have you?" she asked distractedly.

"Have I what?"

She cleared her throat and, fearing that he'd think she was deliberately leaning into him, drew back an inch. "Visited any of those places?"

"No. The places my research takes me are usually more remote. But I'd like to see those cities some day."

She sighed and glanced out to sea. "I'm sure you will. You're much more confident than I am. You can go where you want." She pointed. "See that rock, the one sticking up about halfway between Pride and that island over there?"

"I thought that was a ball buoy."

"Bell buoy, and it is. Not that. Look farther to your right."

He ducked his head so that it was next to hers and followed her line of sight. "The one with the three bulges?"

"That's it. Those three bulges are the proverbial tip of the iceberg. There's an island that spreads out beneath it. My great-grandfather was shipwrecked there. He was the only one of his crew to survive. He washed up on shore here, much the same way we did the other day."

"And your great-grandmother rescued him?"

"She took him in, warmed him up and healed his bruises."

"Then they made a baby." Cameron smiled. "That's nice."

"Not really. He was gone the next day. She had a taste of heaven, then nothing."

"She had the baby, and without that the art of healing would have died with her. What about your grandmother? How did she get *her* baby?"

"A small plane crash-landed in the meadow. It was one of those primitive things, with an open cockpit and propellers that you had to crank up by hand. From what I understand, my grandmother was furious that he'd dared endanger the ponies."

"The ponies were here back then?"

"They were here before people were. There have actually been theories about land masses breaking away from Scandinavia and anchoring themselves here with the ponies aboard, but no one knows for sure. The same mystery surrounds their origin as where they go each winter."

"But they were in the meadow when your grandfather landed, so it must have been summer. Were any of them hurt?"

Summer shook her head, feeling the rub of her French braid against the chambray of his shirt. "No. Grandmother just hated the threat."

"Was your grandfather hurt?"

"Not enough to keep him from seducing my grandmother, then taking off the next day."

"She never saw him again?"

"Nope."

Cameron chuckled against Summer's shoulder. "So you VanVorn women specialize in one-night strands?"

"Stands," she corrected and tried to take offense, but she knew that none had been intended. "It seems to be our fate in life—uh, *their* fate. It ends with me. I'm not going in for any one-night stand."

"Then how will you get your baby?"

"Maybe I won't."

"But if the art dies with you, the island will be without a healer."

"It's bound to happen anyway one of these generations. The skill isn't what it was in my great-grandmother's day. It's getting weaker and weaker."

"I don't know about that. You helped the Shutter baby."

"I gave Morgan medicine. I don't know that it helped."

"I do. I asked Ezra at the store yesterday."

Summer was appalled. "You didn't." She pictured the havoc such a question might cause. "No one but the Shutters was supposed to know they came to me."

"No one does," Cameron assured her, "but before Ezra found out I was with you, he was quite chatty. He wanted to know who I was and when I'd arrived, and in the process of the discussion, I said that I'd overheard someone say the baby was sick. He claimed the child had a rough night but was doing much better that morning, and *all*, Ezra stated quite pointedly, without the help of the healer."

Summer might have figured Ezra would say something like that. "He must have died when he realized you knew me," she said with a touch of perverse pleasure.

"Probably. But, see, you did help that baby. So you're doing something right. You should have more faith in yourself, Summer."

She sighed. "Mmm." But it was a halfhearted agreement, and he knew it right off.

"Why don't you?"

"Because I can't come close to doing what my ancestors did."

"They believed in their power. Maybe that was the secret."

She shook her head. "No. There's more. Somewhere back in the progression of VanVorn women, there was a real source of power. Pure power. But it's been diluted by mating with men who lack that power."

"Do you really think so?"

"It makes sense."

"Maybe. But I still think it has to do with believing. Look at you. Thanks to television and radio and books, you're bombarded with news of modern medicine and scientific findings and technological wizardry. When was the last time you heard anything in praise of folk medicine?"

She couldn't think of a time.

"See? You've been brainwashed into thinking that those other things are stronger and better," he went on, "and consequently you have less faith in your own art. My guess is that if you set your mind to it, you could be just as powerful as the VanVorn women who came before."

Summer liked what he was saying—and the way he was saying it, as though he believed it was true.

"And if that's so," he continued, sitting forward just enough to bring their bodies into contact, "you'd be doing the world—and those VanVorn women—a great disservice by letting the line end. You really ought to think of having a baby."

Summer could have sworn she felt a movement in her womb. It was tiny, little more than a twitch, but in its wake something seemed to be missing. "I'm not sure I want one," she said quietly. Her eyes were lowered, focusing on the rocks. She didn't move away from Cameron. "I'm not sure I want the responsibility of raising a baby alone."

"And there's another example of brainwashing," he said, but his voice was gentle and his mouth warm by her hair. "In the old days, men were off for years at a time fighting wars or hunting whales or transporting cargo to ports on the far side of the world. Women raised babies alone all the time. Suddenly now, in the days of women's liberation, when women are supposedly stronger and more able, raising babies alone isn't good enough. You could raise a child perfectly well, Summer. You could raise a child as well as most two-parent couples. It's simply a matter of believing in yourself."

She let out a tight laugh. "It's more than that. There's the matter of *making* the baby."

"I could help with that," he said, and for a minute, she couldn't breathe. All she could do was shake her head against his shoulder. "Why not?"

"Because it would hurt."

"You're a virgin then?"

Her cheeks flamed; she tucked her chin lower so that he didn't see them. "That's not what I mean. I mean, it would hurt to do that and then have you leave."

He didn't say anything at first. She was beginning to think that she'd done it, that she'd said the one thing that would *make* him leave, when he murmured, "You could leave with me."

She shook her head more convulsively this time. "I couldn't. I couldn't survive away from here."

"Sure you could."

"I wasn't meant to."

"How do you know?"

"I know. I'm not good with people."

"Who's talking people? I'm talking me."

"But you don't live in a vacuum. You work and have friends. I'd be lost in your world."

"Not if you were willing to try it. You could do it, Summer, I know you could." The arm that had been bracing her back slid around it, drawing her closer. "I'd take care of you."

But VanVorns weren't taken care of. They were independent and self-sufficient. And they had responsibilities. Even aside from the issue of providing medicinal preparations for the islanders, there was the meadow. "I couldn't leave here. The ponies need me."

"The ponies would survive."

"If I'm not here to keep buyers away?"

"They'd survive."

But she shook her head, and Cameron didn't argue further. Rather, he moved his hand on her arm, lightly stroking the tension from it. She tried to fight, to tell herself that she couldn't afford to relax against him, but the warnings were useless. His touch had always affected her, and did so even more now.

Waves of pleasure slipped softly through her veins. As they spread through her body, she felt herself grow warm and pliant. She took a slow, deep breath. It was the most natural thing in the world to turn into him as she released it, likewise to make a small sound of pleasure. Her cheek came to rest against his neck, nose against his throat, and the honest maleness of his scent carried the relaxation one step further.

Summer could have stayed just as she was, curled against Cameron's large body forever. The sense of peace she felt was that strong. Also strong was the sense of familiarity—the same one she'd felt before, looking at his face—only this time it spoke of a homecoming.

Then he tipped up her chin, her eyes met his, and the homecoming flared into something both inevitable and predestined. He looked at her mouth. He caressed it with his eyes, then his thumb. Then he lowered his head and touched his own mouth to it.

*Don't,* Summer thought, *please don't,* but in the next moment she was entranced. The feel of his mouth was strange, new, pleasant, exciting. At first, he did nothing more than touch, as though he didn't know what he'd find, but he must have liked that first touch, because when he came back for a second, he was bolder. His mouth not only touched but moved. In the next breath, it opened. In steps, it began to taste and suck and nibble, and with each she grew weaker. Her lips fell open, her breath came shallowly. She was being eaten alive, and she loved it.

His tongue joined in then, tracing the shape of her mouth before venturing inside. She should have been shocked, but the silkiness of it thrilled her. So rather than pulling back, she gave in to the pleasure and let him have his way.

His way was incredibly gentle and increasingly bold. He swept through her mouth, dancing around her tongue until the need to be touched there, too, had her trembling. At the very moment when she might have protested his cruelty, he gave her what she wanted. She barely had time to sigh into his mouth when she caught her breath. For he had slipped a hand between their bodies and was touching her breast.

Her protest this time, taking the form of a short, high sound in her throat, was one of fear. She was burning. The heat was too much. Any more and she'd be scalded, she knew, and tried to convey that to Cameron. He seemed to hear, because his hand slid lower to her waist.

She was feeling joint senses of loss and relief when that hand rose again, this time under her shirt, over her bare skin.

She tore her mouth from his and managed a breathy, "Cameron!"

"I've been wanting to touch you here so badly," he whispered as his fingers traced the contours of her breast. "You were made for my hand. See?"

She couldn't see because her eyes were shut tight against the pain of desire. Nor could she pull away or tell him to stop, and even less so when his mouth claimed hers again. She gave it to him openly, feeling a sudden and intense need for more, and was grateful when he shifted and put a second hand under her shirt so that both breasts could be loved at once. She needed that. Her flesh was swollen, her nipples painfully hard. Only Cameron's touch could soothe the ache.

She was falling, falling hard, falling fast. Instinctively she reached to save herself by wrapping her arms around his neck. She was barely aware that she had left the rock and was standing between his legs, or that her hips were pressed intimately to his. Her body had a mind of its own. It was driven by something stronger than anything she had ever known.

He kept kissing her. He kept touching her. He slid a hand to her bottom and moved her against him, and when that didn't seem enough, he set to unbuttoning her blouse.

"Cameron?" she whispered.

*Trust me,* he said in a silent voice, and it wasn't so much a matter of trust that made her let him open her blouse, as the dire feminine need that had taken command. That need was holding her body away from his just enough to give him the room he needed.

Through a haze of passion, she felt the last of the buttons go, felt the fabric spread apart, felt the warm air on her heated skin. Then she heard his voice.

"Look, Summer."

She didn't want to look, didn't want to see, didn't want to think. She didn't want to be Summer VanVorn, with her special powers that weren't really so special and those other flaws that made her different. She wanted to be Julia Roberts, or Kim Bassinger, or any other alluring woman she'd ever seen on the television screen. She wanted to be sexy. She wanted to be fulfilled.

"Look, sweetie," he said in a voice rough as gravel. "See what we're like together."

The voice broke into her concentration, which was centered on his hands, which were cradling her breasts with a thumb on each nipple. She tried to ignore it, tried to blot out all but the heavenly feel of his hands on her, but the image of what he'd said had taken root and wouldn't be shaken.

She did wonder what they were like together. She wondered about it more and more with each devastatingly light brush his thumbs made, until the wondering itself became an intrusion. So she opened her eyes and looked, and what she saw was riveting. His fingers were long, lean and tanned against her pale skin. As she watched, they moved under and over her breasts, seeming to make them fuller with each turn. She was trying to understand the why of that when he began to tug at her nipples. As gentle as the motion was, it made her cry out.

"What is it?" he whispered against the curve of her ear.

"Hot," she whispered brokenly. "Like fire. A flash of it. Inside."

"Here?" He slid his hand over the front of her jeans, stopping just shy of her crotch.

She grabbed his hand to keep it from going lower, and pressed it tightly to her stomach. With her forehead against his neck, she took in short gasps. She leaned closer, erasing the space between them, preventing any further stroking of her breast.

Very slowly, the intense heat she'd felt ebbed to a more manageable simmer, and the reality of what was happening sank in. Her gasps quieted. So did Cameron's, she realized, and only then recalled the rapid thunder of his heart. There was some consolation in that, and in the force of the erection she'd felt straining against her.

He wanted her. She wanted him. She didn't know what to do.

At a loss for words, she took a deep, shaky breath and let it out in a whoosh. She untangled her hands from the back of his neck and leaned away from him just enough to button her blouse without making a show of it. When that was done, she stepped back.

Cameron took her face in his hands and said with feeling, "If you think that would have been any better with Julia Roberts or Kim Bassinger, you really *are* nuts."

So he'd read her mind. It didn't surprise her. He was unreal in so many other ways that one more was nothing. What was real was the fact that she didn't want him to leave.

"Hey," he said more gently, "why so sad? I'm not leaving yet."

"How do you *do* that?" she asked.

"Do what?"

"Read my mind."

He grinned. "That's my alien half at work. Like it?"

"No, I don't like it," she grumbled. "It's an invasion of my privacy."

"That's your earth half speaking. Earth people are obsessed with keeping secrets."

She wanted to tell him he was absolutely nuts when, in fact, with his midnight blue eyes and his lopsided grin, he was positively adorable. Quite helplessly, because he made her feel good whether he was leaving or not, she gave a lopsided smile of her own. "I promised I'd show you the island. There's a cave not far from here where a person can whisper at one end and be heard loud and clear at the other. Want to try it?"

His eyes widened. His hands fell to her shoulders. "A pirate-type cave?"

"Well, I don't know if it was ever used by real live pirates, but there are bats there."

His eyes widened more. "That's what you need in the meadow. Forget cow dung. Think bats. Better still, I'll think bats while you think cow dung. We'll drive those buyers away by hook or by cook!"

# 6

FRIDAY WAS FOR CARROTS, but only until two in the afternoon. That was when Summer was scheduled to meet with the selectmen of the Isle of Pride.

Together, she and Cameron walked into town. There hadn't been any discussion of his accompanying her. It was simply taken for granted that he would, and not, on Summer's part, for the sake of helping her cause, since she was convinced that the selectmen's minds were already set. But she and Cameron had become a pair. It astounded her to think it, since she was so used to being alone, but they worked well together. She had come to accept—no, more, to anticipate and appreciate—his company. She knew he would leave and that it would hurt when he did, but somehow she had set that thought aside. She had come to think of him as a completion. She felt full when she was with him.

What was it they said, she wondered with a distracted smile, about it being better to have loved and lost than never to have loved at all?

She wondered how Cameron would mess up *that* one.

"Shame on you," he teased as he walked beside her, "thinking thoughts like that."

"Like what?"

"Like the one behind that knowing smile."

"That knowing smile," she improvised, "is in anticipation of your meeting the selectmen. They're like no other governing body you've ever seen."

"I wouldn't be so sure of that," he said and on they walked.

The board of selectmen met at the inn, in the same room that was alternately used for meetings of the Pride Historical Society, the Beautification Committee and the Cemetery Committee, for Christmas parties sponsored by the local fishermen's union and for the reading of wills and other legal matters that would be dismally boring without spicing up. The Barnacle Bar did, indeed, spice things up. Or rather, the bartender did. More accurately, the drinks he served did, and while there was something untoward about the selectmen sitting around a table in a dark corner of the room drinking Jack Daniel's Tennessee Sour Mash Whiskey at two in the afternoon, the picture they made was no different than it had been every other time Summer had appeared before them.

Hapgood Pauling sat on the left, Keegan Benhue in the middle, Oaker Dunn on the right. All three were in their sixties and balding, wore short-sleeved shirts buttoned to the throat and had both hands wrapped around their old-fashioned glasses.

"Summah," Keegan said when Summer and Cameron approached their table, "there's business to do b'fore we talk. Wait outside. We'll call you shortly."

"What business?" Cameron asked when they returned to the lobby. "I don't see anyone else here. They have the bar to themselves. Is there so much local business to attend to?"

"Not likely," Summer said wryly, "considering that they meet three times a week."

"*Three.*"

"It's a great excuse for a private happy hour. The bar is closed to the rest of the town while they meet."

He snorted. "Sly buggers."

"Uh-huh."

"Are these guys elected?"

"Yes, but it's a formality. There's a small in group that consists of the leading families in town. The selectmen always come from that group. They decide among themselves who will serve for a given three-year period. That name is nominated at the town meeting, and the election takes place on the spot. The vote is always unanimous."

Cameron regarded her skeptically. "*You* voted for these guys?"

"Oh, no. I don't go to the town meetings."

"Why not?"

"Because VanVorns never do."

"Why?" he repeated.

"Because we're outsiders."

"But you *live* here."

"We're still outsiders. I could go if I wanted, I suppose, but I'm not sure it's worth being stared at. I go my own way and do my own thing. Nothing that happens in these meetings affects me much."

"Things relating to the meadow affect you."

"Those aren't decided in town meetings. They are more a social event than anything else. Things to do with the meadow are decided right here. And I know how the selectmen stand. I've met with enough different threesomes over the years. They all agree on the expendability of the ponies."

"Hey!" The bartender called from the door and waved them in.

"That was fast," Cameron said under his breath.

"The delay was for show," Summer explained without rancor. At an early age she had learned that anger was a wasted effort where the selectmen were concerned. "It wouldn't do to let anyone think that they'd taken me right on time." She led the way into the bar.

The selectmen hadn't moved. They must have been planning their offense, though, because all three turned curious eyes on Cameron. Keegan spoke from his spot in the middle. "Is this man with you, Summah?"

"Yes, Keegan."

"You didn't say nothin' about bringin' someone. Is he a relative?"

"No."

"Looks like you. Somethin' in the eyes." He continued to study Cameron. "He isn't a lawyer, is he?"

"As a matter of fact," Cameron injected to Summer's horror, "I am." She shot him a warning glance that he returned with a silent, *Trust me.* Then he faced the trio. "Do you gentlemen have a problem with that?"

Hapgood leaned in from the left and Oaker from the right for a whispered conference. When they straightened, Keegan said, "Don't see the need for no lawyer. This is a friendly meeting."

Cameron smiled. "I'm friendly."

"To who?" Keegan shot back. "If you're thinkin' to come in here an' threaten us with some fool lawsuit, you're no friend of ours."

"There's no lawsuit," Summer said quickly, because the last thing she wanted was to antagonize the selectmen right off the bat.

"Not yet," Cameron cautioned in a judicious voice. "But I must warn you that we are considering filing an application with the Department of the Interior to have the ponies of Pride and their meadow declared a national preserve."

Summer regarded him indulgently. She had been trying for years to get such a declaration, but the government had repeatedly turned down the request.

Keegan drew back his head, tripling his chin. "No reason for that to happen. A meadow's a meadow."

Which was pretty much what the government had said, Summer mused.

"Not this one," Cameron declared. "This one's different."

Hapgood rolled his eyes and muttered something under his breath.

Cameron leaned forward. "I'm sorry. I didn't catch that."

Oaker took a drink.

Keegan cleared his throat. "What Hap said is that Summah's always sayin' the meadow's different, only she can't prove it. If she can't prove it to us, she can't prove it to the U.S. gov'ment, an' if she can't do that, they won't go declarin' anything a preserve." He cleared his throat again. "Now about the OSAY Company." He paused for a drink. Hapgood followed suit. Clearly thinking it the thing to do, Oaker took another swallow.

"The OSAY Company," Keegan began, "is successful folk. They're known all over the country."

"For what?" Cameron asked innocently.

Keegan looked rattled. Summer suspected that his prepared speech didn't allow for interruptions. Furthermore, she suspected that that was what Cameron hoped, and though she didn't think for a minute that it would change the outcome of the meeting, she settled in to watch her champion at work.

It was nice to have someone do the talking for her, particularly someone as sharp as Cameron. She wondered if he did have legal training mixed in with his scientific training. He would make an effective lawyer, charming the jury with a smile. Not that he had exactly charmed the selectmen, but they weren't charmable men.

Keegan nudged Hapgood. "You talked with OSAY. Tell 'em what they're known for."

"I talked with 'em about Pride. Oaker's the one to say what they're known for."

"Oaker?" Keegan prompted.

"Stars," stated Oaker. "They study the stars."

"They're into astrology?" Cameron asked politely.

"A-yuh."

Cameron arched both brows. "Horoscopes?"

Oaker frowned and turned to Keegan. "That don't sound right. Does OSAY do horoscopes?"

"Of course not," Keegan muttered. "Weirdos do horoscopes."

"Astronomy," Hapgood snapped impatiently. "OSAY builds observatories to *watch* the stars. But it don't so much matter what they done in the past, as what they want to do here."

"Hap's right," Keegan said. "The OSAY Company wants to build a satellite tracking station here on the Isle of Pride. They say we're just right for it because of our location."

"And our size," Oaker added.

"And because we don't have smog," Hapgood pointed out.

"Now, a tracking station would be nice," Keegan picked up, "because it don't involve all kinds of dirty work, just a building and some satellite dishes."

"How big?" Cameron asked.

"How big what?"

"The building."

"Real small," Keegan promised. "*Real* small."

"And the satellite dishes?"

"Even *smaller*."

Cameron nodded gravely. He slid his hands into his pockets. Then he turned and strode off to the right. "Then there's no reason they can't be put up on the bluff." He swiveled. "Or in that field behind the cemetery." He started back. "Or down on the far side of the docks." He passed Summer, continuing to her left in that same casual gait. "Come to think of it, that wouldn't be a bad spot at all. The shacks there don't serve any practical purpose." He scratched his head. "Quite frankly, and speaking as one in the know," he added in a voice weighed down with grimness, "I say that they're a liability just waiting to happen."

None of the three men looked as if they understood what he was talking about. Summer wasn't sure she did, nor was she sure how Cameron knew about the field behind the cemetery or the shacks beyond the dock. She hadn't taken him to either of those places. But she had to hand it to him; he certainly sounded authoritative.

It occurred to her that she was enjoying herself.

Not Keegan. "Liability?" he echoed perplexedly.

"Legal liability," Cameron specified. He had turned and was ambling to the right. "Those shacks—you know which ones I'm talking about, don't you?" When the men bobbed their heads, he passed Summer and went on. "Those shacks are dangerous, yet the local children play there every day. All it will take is for one child to topple out of a boarded-up window—" he stopped walking to face the trio "—and Pride will have a major lawsuit on its hands."

"No one'll sue us," Keegan scoffed.

"That's what they all say," Cameron told him and resumed his easy pacing. "But there's big money in personal liability and damage recovery these days. Take my word for it—and I won't even charge you for the advice—you're asking for trouble with those shacks. Besides, they're an eyesore." He paused again, this time by Summer's side. "You want a satellite tracking station on the island? Put it down there. Let the OSAY Company do your dirty work for you."

Oaker snorted. "OSAY don't want to be by the docks, and the fishermen don't want 'em there."

"Well, we don't want them in the meadow," was Cameron's response.

But Keegan shook his head. "The meadow is the best place."

"What about the ponies?" Summer asked. Much as she was enjoying Cameron's show, the ponies were, after all, her first priority.

Keegan sighed. "The ponies will go elsewhere."

"They won't graze elsewhere," she argued as she had so many times before. "They'll only eat the leaves from the beech trees in the meadow."

"Some of the beech trees will be left standing." Proudly, Keegan said, "We specifically told the group they had to leave some."

"How many of the thirty there now?"

"At least ten." Still proudly, Keegan continued, "The group thought they might have just enough room between satellite dishes for that many."

Summer wasn't impressed. "But when that's done, there won't be room for the ponies to graze." She shook her head. "It's unacceptable. It's *unthinkable*."

Keegan leaned forward on his elbows with his eyes narrowed. "Look here, girl, what *you* think don't really matter. We didn't have to invite you here. It was a courtesy we did on the off chance you might listen to reason."

"I'd listen to reason if I heard any," she said, "but you haven't said anything reasonable. The ponies need the beech trees in the meadow. Anywhere else, and the leaves aren't the same. Ten trees won't support the whole band."

"They're not here but three months a year, for cripes sake," Oaker yelled.

"Three months that are critical to their survival," Summer argued.

"So what about the other nine months?" he shot back. "Whadda they eat then?"

Summer had asked herself that question many times, and she still hadn't found the answer. Going without that answer had never been more painful than it was now.

"They eat the fruit of the bunkenberry bush," Cameron said in such a knowledgeable way that even Summer turned to stare. "It's a small, berry type fruit that tends to be more tart in the fall months than it is in winter. By spring it gets sweet, which is what the ponies like best. But then—" he shrugged "—the berries stop growing until fall. That's why the ponies come here."

*Where do they go?* Summer wanted to ask but was loathe to advertise her ignorance before the selectmen.

Keegan had no such qualms. "Where do they go?"

"Oh," Cameron said, sucking in a breath, "wherever they can find the bunkenberry bush."

Keegan scowled at Hapgood. "You ever seen a bunkenberry bush?"

"Nope."

He turned to Oaker. "You?"

Oaker shook his head.

"Where do they grow?" Keegan asked Cameron.

"Not around here, that's for sure. They need a totally different soil composition and air that is far thinner."

"Higher altitude?"

"You could say that."

"Too high to transplant some beech trees?"

"Definitely. The beeches wouldn't survive there any more than the bunkenberries would survive here."

"Might o' known," Keegan grumbled and sat back in his chair. He slid his whiskey glass from one hand to the other and tripled his chin again. "Well, look," he suddenly burst out, "some got to win and some got to lose. I say that the OSAY tracking station will benefit a sight more people on this island than those ponies ever did. There's money coming along with that station, and we need it." He leaned forward again, looking directly at Summer. "Those men are coming to see the meadow on Monday. Always before, whether we tell you they're coming or not, you're out there watchin', and that's when the trouble starts, so I want you to stay away this time."

"If I'm not there, the ponies may get spooked," Summer warned.

"Well, you tell 'em b'forehand *not* to get spooked."

"It doesn't work that way," she said. It had with her mother, who could communicate with the ponies simply by thinking their thoughts, but Summer had lost the knack. "I have to be there."

"Not this time," Keegan commanded.

Cameron stood straighter. "Is that a threat?"

"A-yuh."

"That meadow is in the public domain," Cameron informed him in a courtroom clip. "Summer has just as much right as the next person to be there."

"No, she don't. She's a spoiler."

Ignoring him, Cameron turned to Summer. "This man's attempt to restrict your movement is an infringement of the rights granted you in the First Amendment to the Bill of Rights, which specifically states that you may assemble peaceably on public land."

"Peaceably!" Oaker roared, having drained his Jack Daniel's. "Hah! She doesn't do it peaceably! She causes all kinds o' mayhem!"

"*She* causes?" Cameron asked, the soft-spoken cross-examiner once more. "Have you proof that *she* causes mayhem?"

"She's there and it happens," Hapgood said. "What more proof do you need?"

"The court needs much more. The court needs very concrete proof, proof that will convince a jury beyond a shadow of a doubt that she, and she alone, causes mayhem. Now, I ask you, sir, have you that proof?"

Hapgood stared at him for a minute. Then he looked at Keegan, who looked at Oaker, who looked right back at Hapgood.

"I rest my case," Cameron announced. Turning to Summer, he gave her a victorious grin.

Summer couldn't help but grin at him. He was absolutely precious. *Lawyer, my foot!*

His eyes twinkled. *What does your foot have to do with it?*

*You're no lawyer! What were you thinking when you said that?*

*I was thinking it'd be fun to pretend.*

*You did sound a little like a lawyer.*

*After watching more than a hundred episodes of* L.A. Law, *I should hope so.*

"Summah VanVorn," Keegan interrupted, looking blustery, "I don't care what this lawyer friend of yours says, if anything happens come Monday to mess up that meadow, we'll hold you personally responsible."

"Please, gentlemen," Cameron said and held up a hand. "No more threats."

"Just keep her away from the meadow on Monday."

"I can do that."

The three went still. "You can?" Hapgood asked.

Cameron nodded.

"But—" Summer began, only to be stopped by the hand he put on her arm.

"*Will* you?" Keegan asked.

"Sure," he said. "Tell you what. I'll stay with her myself and watch her every minute. That way, if something happens, you'll know it wasn't her who did it. Deal?"

Oaker called, "Why sh'we trust you?"

"Because I'm a lawyer," he said as though that was the absolute, definitive answer.

The three men huddled for another whispered conference. It was Hapgood who spoke when they finally straightened. "It's a deal. You stay with her and watch her." His voice rose. "But if there's snakes or bugs or big smelly puddles, we'll know it was her. She's done those b'fore."

"No snakes or bugs or puddles," Cameron said, taking Summer's arm. "I promise."

"I HAVE TO BE THERE," she said as soon as they were on the road again. "The ponies need me."

"To do what?"

"*Be* there."

"But you said you really don't make all those things happen yourself."

"I don't." She frowned. "At least, I don't think I do. I'm not sure."

"What do you mean, you're not sure?"

She tried to explain. "Well, I *want* all those things to happen. I think about them. I pray really hard that they will. And when they do, I begin to think that maybe I have the power after all. Then I try making it work on something else, and it doesn't. So I know it wasn't me." She stopped. "Then again," she said with a new breath, "there's always the tiniest chance that I have *something* to do with it, and if so, do I dare risk the ponies' lives by staying away from the meadow?"

He took her hand and held it gently as they walked. "No risk. I'll take care of it."

"You?"

"Sure. There's more than one way to skin a rat, y'know."

"That's cat. Skin a cat. And I don't follow."

He wove his fingers through hers. "In the past, prospective buyers come here and then run into trouble. What if the people from OSAY can't get here in the first place?"

"Of course they can get here. If they don't want to take the ferry, they can hire a private boat, and if not that, a plane. Come to think of it, a company like that probably already has its own plane."

"But what if they can't get here? What if there's an invisible barrier that won't allow them within five miles of the island?"

She sighed. "You must watch *Star Trek* right along with *L.A. Law*. Cameron, invisible barriers don't happen. Not in real life."

He tsked. "Such a cynic. Where's your sense of imagination?"

"It's nonexistent where the ponies are concerned. When it comes to them, I have to be a realist. The fact is that, to survive, they need the meadow in its present form. My imagination won't save them, and unless something else does, they'll be doomed."

Dropping her hand, he wrapped his arm around her shoulder and pulled her close. "I'll save them. That's what I'm here for."

She pulled away, protesting, "This isn't a joke, Cameron. You may think it is, because you'll be turning around and leaving the island soon. When push comes to shove, you don't care about the ponies."

He looked wounded. "I do, too."

She didn't like that wounded expression. It was too real. So she quickened her pace until she was several steps ahead. Speaking more loudly so that her words would drift back, she said, "They're my responsibility. You had no business telling the selectmen that you'd keep me in the cabin. No business at all." She glared at him over her shoulder. "How can you tell me to sit back and do nothing?"

With no effort at all, he caught up to her and said, "I can tell you that because *I* won't be sitting back and doing nothing. I'll be using my own skill to keep those OSAY men from reaching this island."

"But you can't do that," she cried. "You're not Superman!"

"Almost."

She groaned and walked faster. "You're crazy."

"No more than you. You have certain powers. Well, so do I."

"I *don't* have powers. I *don't!*"

"You would if you believed in yourself. You're having a crisis of confidence, that's all. Not me. I'm prepared to do whatever is necessary to keep those men from coming near the meadow."

She glanced at his face. He was staring straight ahead, wearing a look of grim determination. "You really *are* crazy," she said with a frisson of unease and tore her gaze away. But the unease grew. Since he had carried her from the ocean and taken up residence in her home, he had said some strange things. He had *done* some strange things, if she chose to believe that he'd had a hand in making the Mundy boys cough or making Jeb Strunk fall from his seat. He'd done some *really* strange things, if she chose to believe that he had mended what might well have originally been a crushed kneecap or broken ribs. And then there was the way he played the harpsichord, and the way he spoke to her through his eyes, and the way he touched a spot deep, deep inside her that no one else had ever touched.

Suddenly frightened of what he might be and what that might do to her life, she said, "I want you to leave."

"Come on, Summer."

"I do. You said you would if I asked, and I'm asking. I need time to think."

He caught her arm, forcing her to stop. "I can't leave now. There's too much at stake."

She studied the ground. "I'm asking, Cameron."

"Look at me and ask."

She shook her head. "Your eyes do things. I just want you to leave."

"I promised the selectmen I'd stay."

"You also promised me you'd leave if I asked."

"But what about us?"

"There is no us," she cried, fighting the pain the words brought. "I've been telling you that all along. I don't know where you're from or where you're going, but my life is here. Alone."

"It doesn't have to be."

"It *does*."

He remained silent, standing straight and tall beside her. She felt his warmth over that of the sun, beckoning to her, and the urge to lean into him, to wrap her arms around his waist and beg him to forget what she'd said and stay, was nearly overpowering.

"Please," she whispered, squeezing her eyes shut. "Please leave."

Hands clenched at her sides to keep them from doing anything foolish, she waited for him to speak. Cameron had never been one to stay silent for long. If he didn't express himself in words, he usually found another way to talk.

She waited. After a minute, she started to tremble, but not from the excitement of his nearness. Rather, she felt a sudden chill, a dawning emptiness, a slow-swelling aloneness. With that came an understanding of what had happened. She opened her eyes to confirm it.

Sure enough, Cameron was gone. She looked forward, then back, but there was no sign of him anywhere. She peered into the woods on either side of the road. "Cameron?" she cried, then pressed her hand to her mouth to keep from crying out again.

*You wanted this*, she told herself. *You wanted things back the way they were, now you'll have your wish.* Slowly, she pulled her hand away from her mouth and tucked it into her pocket. She swallowed and started walking, ignoring the tears in her eyes. *It's for the best*, she insisted. *He's too complicated for you. You need a simple life, like your mother's and your grandmother's and your great-grandmother's. VanVorns weren't made to have men around.*

"But what about my baby?" she whispered, then bit her lip so hard it stung.

*You'll do fine without a baby. You wouldn't be much
of a mother, anyway. You'd never be able to teach your
child half of what your mother taught you. You were a
lousy student.*

The tears began trickling down her cheeks. She
brushed them away and repeated the gesture several
minutes later. Pure instinct guided her to the cabin in the
woods. Once there, she climbed to the loft, crawled into
bed, and not caring that it was barely four in the afternoon, cried herself to sleep.

THE CABIN WAS DISMAL without him. She saw him everywhere—playing the harpsichord one minute, watching
television the next, talking with her on the porch or
helping her scrape carrots or massaging her knee the
next. More than once, she smelled the clean male scent
that only in hindsight she identified as his, only to whirl
around expecting to find him and finding emptiness instead. He was everywhere, but nowhere at all.

She had known his leaving would hurt, but she hadn't
known how much. The ache inside was nearly constant.
It defied her attempts to keep busy, whether she was
canning asparagus or corn, whether she was gathering
herbs from the woods, whether she was watching the
ponies. She tried to play it away, first on her pipe, then
on her flute, then on the harpsichord that Cameron had
played so masterfully himself.

Nothing worked. More often than not she ended up
crying, which was so untypical that it only underscored
her loss.

By the time Sunday morning rolled around, she was
desperate. Praying that a change of scenery would help,
she put bits of food into her shoulder bag and set out for
the woods on the far side of the meadow. She hadn't

taken Cameron there. She hadn't taken *anyone* there, not even her mother. It was a secret place from her childhood, a protective nook made of fallen trees and boulders. All Summer wanted was to crawl in and sit, to clear her mind of Cameron, to concentrate on pure, simple thoughts and thereby find a measure of peace.

It worked. The ache inside eased. Her eyes dried. Her muscles relaxed. She crawled out in the early evening to check on the ponies, and the ache returned. So she crawled back in and spent the night, curled in a ball with her head on a bed of moss.

Come morning, she crawled out and settled herself in the midst of a cluster of mountain laurels at the edge of the meadow, from where she could watch without being seen. Yes, her presence would have a calming effect on the ponies. More importantly, though, she would be able to focus her energy on discouraging the men of OSAY from building their tracking station in the meadow. She didn't care what Cameron had promised the selectmen. She couldn't just sit back and do nothing. Given that she had neither a baby nor a lover, protecting the meadow was her sole reason for being.

She sat and waited. Eight in the morning became nine, then ten, and there were no visitors to the meadow. She found herself thinking about cow dung, then bats, then Cameron, and the ache inside her returned. She tried to push it aside, tried to concentrate solely on creating a disaster to turn away the team from OSAY, but the ache kept intruding. She considered returning to her secret nook to recover a bit of peace, but she didn't dare. If she was gone when the men came, there would be no hope of saving the meadow.

Eleven passed, then noon. She sat peering out through a lacework of branches, barely moving, barely breathing. One o'clock came and went and still there were no men, which suggested that they hadn't taken the ferry over from the mainland. She listened for a plane approaching the island, but heard none, which left a chartered boat as the strongest possibility.

Her mind wandered. She wondered where Cameron was and what he was doing. Tears came to her eyes. She pushed them away and concentrated on thinking about large, intricate sticky spiderwebs that might be so repulsive to the men of OSAY that they would turn away in disgust.

No spiderwebs materialized. Neither did the men of OSAY. Two o'clock came, then three, and she grew puzzled. Four came and went, and the meadow remained as quiet as ever, with only the ponies and a gentle breeze stirring the air.

Still Summer didn't move. On the theory that the selectmen might try to trick her by coming later, she stayed hidden in the laurels. The sun lowered in the sky, casting progressively long shadows. Its warmth gave way to an ocean breeze that grew brisker as dusk neared.

Finally, when the light in the meadow was too dim for the selectmen or anyone else but Summer to see, she emerged from her hiding place. She didn't understand what had happened. Keegan had said Monday. She was *sure* he'd said Monday, and more than once. Yet no one had come.

Confused, she started toward the cabin. Midway there, though, she stopped and changed directions. The only things she would find at the cabin, she knew, were memories of Cameron and an ache in her heart. She couldn't go there. Not yet. Not with the mystery of the OSAY men hanging over her head, as well.

So she went into town. She took her time, pretending she was out for a casual walk, but once she arrived, she didn't know what to do. She passed the street where Hapgood Pauling and Oaker Dunn lived with their families, then the street where the Keegan Benhues lived. But she didn't knock on any doors. What could she say? *I was hiding in the bushes and you didn't come. If they're coming another day, let me know when, so I can go back to the laurels and concentrate on sticky spiderwebs again.*

She walked all the way past the docks to the old shacks that Cameron had suggested be razed. Cameron. Last time she'd been in town, she'd been with him. She'd felt safe and protected. She'd felt proud. She'd felt *normal.*

"Oh, God," she whispered when her eyes filled with tears. She pressed an arm across her middle in an attempt to dull the ache there. She missed him. So much.

It seemed forever that Summer stood like that, having lost the will to move. The night was moonless, the shacks before her dark, hulking shadows. Water lapped at the hulls of nearby boats, which in turn creaked against their floats. She might well have been the only person on the island, the sense of desolation that engulfed her was so strong.

Then, in a terrifying instant, she knew she wasn't the only person there at all. Out of the night a pair of arms caught her up in a powerful grip. Her first thought was that Cameron had returned to sweep her out of the gloom, but Cameron's arms had never bitten into her cruelly, as these were doing.

She began to struggle. "Let me go!"

The arms around her tightened, immobilizing her arms, nearly cutting off her breath. "Not real fast," said a coarse voice by her ear, and she felt herself being toted toward the nearest shack.

*Fight!* she cried, but the ease with which she was being carried told her that her abductor was far stronger and larger than she. When she kicked at his legs, she was simply hauled higher against his front in a way that left her kicking at air.

"Thought you was real smart," the voice growled. "Thought y'd fool us into thinkin' y'didn't have nothin' to do with it."

She pinned down his voice. It belonged to Hallard Dunn, Oaker's brother and the town drunk. Only he didn't sound drunk to Summer. He sounded very angry and very purposeful.

"To do—with what?" she managed, trying futilely to thrash her way free. But she was no match for him physically. She would never make it alone.

"Scarin' them off. Don't know how y'did it, but they changed'r minds w'out ever seein' the meadow."

"I don't know—didn't have anything—"

He knocked what was left of her breath away when he thrust her against a wall. His body followed, flattening hers to the splintering wood. He took a painful grip of her chin and muttered through gritted teeth, "Don' talk. Witches don' say the truth. They talk in circles an' then lay their hands on people an' mess things up." He thrust his free hand between them and, while she convulsed in horror, began to maul her breasts. "We needed that station—"

"Don't!" She bucked against him but his body was leaden. *Cameron! I need you, Cameron! Help me! Please!*

"Needed the jobs to build it," he gritted, "an' the business it'd bring later. Now you ruined it." He pushed her shirt up. "So I'm gonna ruin you." His beefy hand contracted on her bare breast.

She screamed.

He covered her mouth. "Shut up! Shut up!" Holding that hand on her mouth, he imprisoned her with his legs while he fumbled with the snap of her jeans.

*Dear God! Cameron!*

"They wouldn't come, witch. Said they had a bad feelin' about the place. Said there's too many stories about th'island bein' haunted." He got her zipper down and fumbled with his own. "Who told 'em those stories, witch? *Who told 'em?*"

"I did!" came a belligerent roar from behind, and before its echo had died, Hallard had been hauled off her and thrown to the side.

# 7

SUMMER CRUMBLED against the wall with her knees to her chest and her arms over her head. She was shaking all over, breathing in terrified spurts at the sound of fist hitting flesh.

It seemed to go on forever. She heard grunts and groans and covered her head more tightly. Needing to escape but unable to stand, she pushed herself backward until she reached the corner and another wall. Turning toward it, she huddled into an even smaller ball. If she'd been able, she would have shrunk to nothing at all and disappeared.

But she didn't have that power.

Suddenly, with a final grunt, a final blow and the final thud of a weighty body going inert, all was still. In the next instant, Cameron lifted the small bundle that she was into his arms and carried her quickly away from the shack, then the docks, then the center of town. He didn't speak, and neither did Summer. She was shaking all over, gasping for air between the silent sobs that racked her.

His steps were long and steady. In no time, the town had been left behind and they entered the forest. The smell was different here, more pine than salt, and that combined with Cameron's scent to work its way through her. Little by little she uncoiled from her tight ball and turned into him. She buried her face against his chest, then his throat when her arms crept around his neck.

He carried her into the cabin, went straight through to the bathroom and turned on the shower. With infinite care, he propped her against the sink, took her face in both hands and tipped it to his. He wiped her eyes with his thumbs, which were exquisitely gentle in comparison to his voice. "I could have killed that bastard," he whispered harshly, "killed him." He took a shuddering breath. Through her tears, his face looked tormented. "But he'll live to remember what he tried to do and what'll happen to him if he ever tries to do it again. Now all I want is to wash his filth from your body." The steam from the shower had started to fill the room. He shot a glance at the stall. When he faced her again, his voice was softer. "Should I leave?"

"No!" she cried. The thought was inconceivable. Circling his waist with her arms, she held on with a strength she hadn't had moments before. "Don't leave. Not now. Not again. It was bad enough before. Don't do it again." She didn't know what had brought him back, didn't know where he'd been or how he'd known to find her at the docks just when she'd needed him most, but he had, and she wasn't sending him away again. If he went, he would be the one to decide it.

He kissed her forehead, then her eyes, her nose and her cheeks. He couldn't kiss her mouth because she was crying again, making soft keening sounds this time. All she wanted was to bury herself against him and stay there forever.

But he wouldn't allow it. Carefully he undressed her, taking off first her shirt, then her sneakers, jeans and panties. His own clothes were off in the next instant. Gently he helped her into the shower, came in right with her and took the soap.

His touch was healing. He covered those places Hallard had, washed away the dirt and eased the bruises. He built up a lather and covered every inch of her with it, then rinsed her off and lathered her again. She should have been embarrassed by the intimacy, but she wasn't. Her body was his. She should have known it all along.

When the water started to cool, he reached behind her and turned it off. Frightened, because she remembered the emptiness and the aloneness all too well, she clung to his neck. "You won't leave me now, will you?" she whispered.

"Never, sweetie," he whispered back. Taking a towel, even while she held on, he dried her with the same gentle care with which he had undressed her and washed her. After he'd dried himself, he picked her up again. This time he carried her up the stairs to the loft. After he'd pulled back the bedclothes and set her there, he stretched out beside her and, with the lamp from below casting a pale and shadowy glow, drew her close.

"Oh Cameron," she whispered. She looked at the dark spikes of his damp hair, at the darker blue of his eyes, at the strong lines of his cheeks and his nose and his chin. She loved him so much. "I shouldn't have sent you away like that." Needing to touch him, she put one hand around his neck, the other on his chest. "I don't know why I did. I was scared, I guess."

"Scared of me?" he murmured.

"And of what I was feeling."

"Are you now?"

She thought back to the ache of being without him and her eyes widened in fear. "I'm only scared that you won't love me." She reached for his hand and brought it to her breast. The gesture was artless, but she didn't care; the sensation it created was so pleasurable that she had to close her eyes for a minute before she could speak. "I need you, need you so badly, Cameron. I've never needed another person like this. Please love me."

He made a strained sound and came over her in a way that made it clear she wasn't the only one in need. Twining her fingers with his, he pinned them to the sheet by her shoulders and began to kiss her as he'd done before, first her forehead, then her eyes, her cheeks and her nose. When he reached her mouth, it was open and waiting for him just as the rest of her body was, and if that knowledge should have been cause for dismay, Summer refused to let it be so. Independence was fine. So were self-sufficiency and self-containment. But being with a man this way, loving him this way, was every bit as fine. If he left in the future, so be it, but until then she would know what it was to be loved.

His kiss ate at her until she was dizzy with wanting. She had her fingers in his hair by then, hanging on, holding him close. Both became more important than ever when he lowered his head to her breast.

She arched off the bed at the pleasure of it. Her skin, already warmed by the shower, took on a fevered glow, while the heat spread inside.

He raised his head. *You're beautiful*, said his eyes, which were the deepest, darkest, most velvety blue she'd ever seen. *I love you.*

"Don't stop," she whispered urgently and ran her fingertips over his face. "Don't stop."

He covered her lips with a kiss that left her breathing as hard as he was. "This really wasn't supposed to happen," he said in an amused, if ragged, tone, "but I do love you." He kissed her again, and at the same time slid a hand down her body. His fingers slipped easily through the pale curls at the apex of her thighs, then slipped deeper.

She sighed into his mouth.

"This would have frightened you last week," he whispered against her lips.

The delight was rising, heat gathering and radiating. "Mmm."

"It doesn't now?"

"Oh, no." To the contrary, it felt so right—more so than anything else in recent memory. Without conscious thought, she opened her legs to his touch.

"Tell me what it's like," he asked. He was on an elbow beside her, his free hand smoothing wisps of damp blond hair from her face.

She opened her eyes to see his need. "It's like—" She tried to think, but the undulation of his fingers made it difficult. "It's like you touch," she gasped, "touch my whole body when you do that. Everything swells."

"And when I do this?" he asked, stroking deeper.

She sucked in a breath.

"Good?" he whispered.

"Yes." She gulped.

"And this?" He slipped a finger inside.

"Ooh."

Then another.

"*Cameron.*" She closed her eyes and swung her head against the pillow.

He put his mouth to her ear. "Do you remember that night?"

"What night?" She could barely think, much less remember.

"When I played the harpsichord?" His fingers were moving rhythmically, stretching her slowly, gently, entering her more and more deeply. "I made love to you

then with my music. I hadn't meant to, but I needed you
so badly that it just happened."

His words were a blur, barely audible past the heat
throbbing through her veins.

"Summer?"

She moved her hips to urge a deeper penetration.
"Hmm?"

"Open your eyes."

She struggled to do it, finally seeing him through a
haze of passion.

"When we made love then," he said in the softest
murmur above a whisper, "it wasn't the physical kind
we'll be making now. It was just as real, but not physical, so you're still technically a virgin. That means I have
to hurt you for a minute, just for a minute." His fingers
grew purposeful. She felt a sharp twinge inside, but before she could tell him about it, he explained, "That was
your maidenhead. I had to break it, but it's healing now."
His fingers were moving in a soothing way, and sure
enough, the pain was little more than a memory. In fact,
his thumb was brushing over her in a way that was
building her need again.

When the need grew urgent, she grabbed his wrist and
pulled his hand from her. "Make love to me," she begged,
rolling over until her body was pressed to his. He was
fully aroused. Driven by a need so consuming that if
she'd had any inhibitions left they would have been shed,
she raised her thigh over his.

He groaned and stiffened. "How did you know to do
that?"

"The movies. Hurry, Cameron. I need you."

He smiled. "This much?" The smallest movement of
his hips brought an initial penetration that left her aching.

"More," she whispered and, clutching his lean back-side, pulled him closer. She felt the flex of his muscles as he pushed deeper, but still it wasn't enough.

"*Please*, Cameron," she pleaded.

He rolled her to her back then, rose over her and entered her so smoothly and conclusively that a high cry broke from her throat. She arched, head back and breasts thrust toward him. All it took was the single touch of his tongue to a pebbled nipple to catapult her into a new, brilliantly hot and exquisitely pure realm of pleasure.

Her orgasm was endless. Spasms shook her inside and out, and it seemed that with his own triumphant cry, they started again. She had never in her life felt anything as intensely beautiful as his life force filling her. Her final thought before she gave herself up to the glory of it was that if a baby came, it would be a very precious gift.

LATER, basking in the afterglow of what they'd shared, Summer held him tightly. She was lying half over him, with one arm around his neck and the other across his chest. She didn't think she'd ever let him go—or be let go, for that matter. His arm was wrapped every bit as snugly around her.

"Cameron." His name was little more than an expiration of breath, an excuse to move her mouth against his skin. He had wonderful skin. It was firm and smooth, except where he had hair, and that was so manly that she couldn't complain. She slid her hand over him, adoring both the smooth and the textured.

"You okay?" he whispered against her forehead.

"Oh, yes," she whispered back, smiling. The smile had barely faded, though, when her eyes filled with tears and the horror of earlier—not the attack at the dock, but the weekend's despair—broke through her languor. "I thought you were gone, really gone. I thought I'd never see you again."

"How could that happen? Didn't you guess how I felt about you?"

She tipped her head to see his face. "No. But say it now. Say it again."

"I love you."

"No one's ever told me that before."

"Not your mother?"

"My mother doesn't count. I mean a man."

"Well, I'm saying it now, and it's true. Did you honestly think I'd just disappear?"

"You did!" She remembered how they had stood on the road and he had been there one minute and gone the next. "You disappeared into thin air."

"Because you asked me to go. But I'd have been back. I was actually back this morning, only you weren't at the cabin."

And he was! She thought of the pain she'd felt that day, all unnecessary. "I was hiding in the bushes watching the meadow." She came up on his chest, propping herself on a forearm. "The men never showed, Cameron. I sat there all day, and they never came. I stayed until it got dark, then started back here, but I didn't want to be in the cabin without you, so I walked into town."

His expression tightened. "And got accosted."

Now she allowed herself to recall that attack, including what Hallard had said just before Cameron had come. In a hushed voice, she asked, "Did you really tell those people that the meadow was haunted?"

"I sure did. I told you there were other ways to keep them away from here. You didn't like my idea of setting up a barrier around the island to prevent them from reaching it, and the more I thought of it, the more I realized you were right. They wouldn't understand what was happening. Nothing in their experience would explain their inability to get through. So they'd just keep trying. Either that, or they'd make such a big fairy deal—"

"Hairy, not fairy."

"—about supernatural goings-on here that they'd have the national news media on their case. It occurred to me to be more subtle and just make them change their minds about coming in the first place."

Summer pushed herself up and folded her legs. Her knees still touched his thigh—she couldn't completely sever the connection—but her hands were tucked in the sheets in her lap. Words came to her then, words that she had pushed from her mind in the pain of missing Cameron. She remembered the argument they'd had after meeting with the selectmen. He had said strange things, and she had been frightened. So she'd asked him to leave.

"How did you get them to change their minds?" she asked guardedly.

"Just like that bastard said," he announced. "I convinced them the meadow was haunted."

"But how did you do it?"

"I told them about the snakes, the bugs and the puddles. I even threw in a few bats." His lips twitched. "And some cow dung."

"This isn't funny," she said gravely. She could see that he was trying to lighten things up by joking, but the time for that was done. She had given Cameron her heart and soul. Now she needed the truth from him. "*How* did you tell them? Did you arrange a meeting?"

"No."

"Then how?"

Pushing a pillow against the headboard, he propped himself higher. When that was done, he looked at her.

"Tell me, Cameron," she said softly.

After another minute, fully somber now and almost with regret, as though he didn't want to tell her but had to, he said, "I communicated directly with their minds. I planted thoughts there. The thoughts took root. The men met and shared those thoughts and decided that the project was going to be sensitive enough without having to deal with weird happenings."

*Ha, ha, very funny,* she wanted to say, but once too often she had put him off that way. She swallowed. "You communicated directly with their minds."

"Like I do with you."

To prevent him from doing it again, she dropped her gaze to her hands. "Planting thoughts in people's minds isn't normal."

"Not for humans. It is for other species. For some that's their major form of communication."

She did look at him then, studied him closely, trying to see something about him that was nonhuman. But his body was real. It was warm. His hair was human hair, his skin human skin. He ate like humans did and breathed like humans did. Lord knew he made love like humans did. At least she thought so. Never having made love before, she could only guess.

"I do," he said, reading her mind. "My physical response to you is entirely human. In this body, I'm a man like any other on this planet."

"But in another body . . ." She breathed and started to tremble.

"Another form," he corrected and reached for her, but she was off the bed before he could capture her.

She stood in a corner of the loft, shaking. "You're an alien."

"Not to you. To you I'm Cameron. You know me better than anyone ever has."

"But you're from s-somewhere else."

He nodded.

She struggled to take it in, to absorb the fact that the absurd was real, but her mind was a jumble. "It can't be," she murmured, shaking her head in a last attempt at denial. "Aliens don't come to earth. They don't become human and have relationships and have . . . have sex!"

"We didn't have sex," Cameron said in the maddeningly calm way he had of speaking. "We made love. And aliens do love, perhaps even better than humans." He kicked back the sheets and started to climb out of bed.

"Don't you come near me!" she cried, holding out a hand to ward him off.

"I want to hold you, Summer. I need that right now."

She backed up, but her head hit the sloping rafter. "You scare me! Don't—Cameron, don't!" But he had her wrapped in his arms and drawn against his body before she could duck away this time.

"Please, sweetie," he begged so softly that she wondered if he was speaking aloud, "don't be frightened. I'm still me. I still love you."

With her eyes closed and only the strength of his hold, the protectiveness of his stance and the warmth and scent of his body to guide her, she began to relax. "This is so strange."

"Don't you think it is for me, too? I came to earth with a mission, and it didn't include falling in love with you. We have strict rules of conduct back home. I'm afraid I've broken more than one of those rules. But I do love you, Summer."

She turned her face into his chest and, through the swirls of hair there, said, "I should have known something was odd when you swam all that way through the ocean with me. We weren't near Pride. We weren't *anywhere* near Pride."

"Would you have believed me if I'd told you then?"

"No. And my injuries—what was really wrong with me?"

"You'd broken some ribs, fractured your skull and crushed your kneecap."

She'd suspected all but the fractured skull. "How did you heal them?"

"I set my mind to recomposing the broken elements."

"And you put me to sleep that night."

"You needed the rest."

"You made the Mundy boys cough and Jeb Strunk fall. You even made my knee throb when you were trying to convince me to let you help with the harvest."

"I'd never harvested anything before. I wanted to try, and it was fun. Mostly what was fun, though, was being with you."

She groaned. When he said things like that, her heart swelled with love, and when that happened, it didn't seem to matter that he was from an alien world. She wanted him however he was.

Lifting her head, she whispered, "Make love to me again."

As she watched, his face came alive. "You want me to?"

She nodded and inched away enough so that she could look down his body. He was strikingly male and, in that, beautiful.

"I'm glad you think so," he said and took her face in his hands, "or it wouldn't be worth it, running around here in human get-up. It's much more cumbersome than what I usually wear."

"And what's that?" she asked with a smile against his lips, because the business of being an alien was seeming unreal again. The only thing she could relate to was his very large, very male body, and the titillating prospect of his possession.

"A sparkle of white."

"White?"

"I'm one of the good guys."

"Is that so?"

"Yup. I do good deeds. Here. Let me show you." He guided her to the bed and sat her on her heels by the pillows. Then he went to the foot of the bed and faced her. Nearly five feet of bedclothes separated them.

"But I want you to hold me," she cried. Only by touch and feel could she know that he was a man. And by look, she amended. Certainly by look. Standing before her, with his hard, tapering body unclothed, he was spectacular. Still she wanted the holding.

"I will," he assured her. His eyes grew darker, his voice lower. "I am."

She was about to protest when something happened. He was apart from her, his shoulders back and his arms by his sides, nothing about him moving, yet she felt his touch. Clear as day, warm as flesh, sweet as syrup boiled thick and dark, she felt it. It was in a kiss that leisurely laved her lips and left them parted and moist, and in a caress that closed her eyes. It lingered at her throat until, with a sigh, she dropped her head back, then it loved her breasts until her nipples were hard and her torso arched. It moved lower still to her belly and her hips, exploring her curves until she began to writhe, then even lower, until she was gasping for breath against the fire raging between her legs.

Nearly consumed by it, she cried his name, but at that moment his touch abruptly left her. Stunned, she swayed. The rise of passion had made her skin damp; the frustration of near completion had it tingling. Snatching a ragged breath, she opened dazed eyes.

That was when he went to her. Coming down on a knee on the bed, he crawled the short distance and captured her mouth as he bore her down to the sheets. His skin was as damp and hot as hers. He was magnificently erect.

In one fluid motion he was inside her, then thrusting, and though she was untutored in love, she caught his rhythm as though it was an extension of her heartbeat. And in a sense it was, certainly at that moment, for it was as necessary to her existence as the other.

Primed as she'd been, her rise to the edge of orgasm was speedy, but there he held her, withdrawing at the very moment when she thought she'd explode, filling her again once the intensity had ebbed. She was frustrated, but the pleasure of even that was nearly beyond bearing. She enhanced it more by touching him, and in that found his weakness. He didn't last long under the intimate sweep of her hand, and when she approached her peak this time, he didn't have the wherewithal to pull out. Her climax had barely begun when he joined her there, and when the throbbing of their bodies finally eased to a gentler hum, he was as limp, damp and sated as she.

In that warm afterglow she didn't think of him as alien at all, but humanly male through and through. He was a solid presence, just as he'd always been, and his seed was alive inside her.

She clung to that thought, eventually dozing off. When she awoke, though, there were other thoughts that would be no longer denied.

"Cameron?" she whispered. He had awoken soon after her, if the stirring of the heartbeat by her ear was a fair measure.

"Mmm?"

"Tell me where you're from." In the past he'd been vague and said north, so she'd assumed Canada. Clearly she'd assumed wrong.

In a calm, factual voice that told her he understood what she needed to know, he said, "I'm from a planet called Cyteron. It's part of a solar system in the Naquerion Galaxy."

The Naquerion Galaxy. She had never heard of it. Not that that meant anything. "Is it very far from here?"

"Six galaxies. Not so far."

She started to tremble. Disgusted with herself, she whispered, "Why am I shaking?"

"You're hearing the truth and it frightens you."

"It sure does." She gave a high-pitched, slightly hysterical laugh. "I'm lying here with a creature from outer space, with whom I just made love. For all I know, I may be carrying his baby."

"You are."

Her head came up. The trembling increased. "How do you know?"

His eyes were as deep as the sea. "I just know."

But she wanted to know how. "Can you see it?"

"No. I feel it. I hear it."

"Oh, God." She put a hand on her stomach. "What will I give birth to? A little white sparkle?"

"That depends where you are. If you're here you'll give birth to a little boy who'll have your hair and my eyes."

"Oh, God," she said again because she could see it so clearly. "A little boy. Not a girl. You're sure?"

He nodded.

She settled against him again, thinking that there had never been a VanVorn male. In that sense, history wasn't repeating itself at all. Then she caught herself. Of *course* history wasn't repeating itself. None of the VanVorn women had mated with an alien!

She looked at him again, needing the reassurance that his earthly appearance hadn't changed. "Tell me more. How did you get here?"

"I flew."

He had said that before, and she'd misinterpreted him. She didn't now. "You came in a spaceship?"

"That's right."

"Where's the spaceship now?"

"On VanVornland."

Startled, she asked, "How do you know about VanVornland?"

He smiled. "I was watching you there. You were so beautiful, running along the beach with your hair flowing behind you." He wove his fingers through the silken strands, but gingerly, as though he feared they might break. "I saw you leave the island that morning and knew you were headed for trouble. So I followed you, then caught you when your boat was wrecked and you went under."

"Then you didn't have a boat of your own."

"No. That was the only untrue thing I told you, and it bothered me doing that. Where I come from, honesty is revered."

"Is that why you told the selectmen you were a lawyer?" she asked because she couldn't resist.

"That was just play," he said, but apologetically. "I mean, watching lawyers on television makes you want to try it."

"Who inspired you to take on Hallard Dunn?" she asked with a shudder.

He cupped her shoulder, drawing her closer. "You did. I'd have done anything to save you." He paused, then confessed, "The technique was Charles Bronson."

She moaned. It was either that or laugh, and she couldn't laugh in the middle of such a serious discussion. "Is that how you learn about earth culture, by watching television?"

"And movies. And by reading endlessly. We also learn a lot from debriefings of Cyteronians who've spent time here."

"There are others of you?"

"Sure. Some of them are Cyteronians two or three times removed."

"Mixed breeds?"

He nodded. "Actually, that's what brought me to Earth. I really am a research scientist. I'm studying the effects of intermarriage on my people. There are scatterings of us all over the universe. Earth is only a small part of the study."

"Don't tell me," she said because she too had watched *Star Trek*, "Cyteron is in the path of an asteroid that will one day destroy it, so you're looking for the best place to recolonize."

He sighed. "Sorry. No asteroid. We're doing research because we're curious. That's all."

Lying against him, with the strong and steady beat of his heart comforting the part of her that was frightened, Summer let his words sink in. On the one hand they were incredible and not to be believed for a minute. On the other hand they made perfect sense.

"Well?" he finally asked. "What do you think?"

"I think that the more I know, the less I know. Did you have a human form when you were traveling in your spaceship?"

"No. I wouldn't have fit."

"Because we're more cumbersome." He'd said that before. "When did you change?"

"When I left the spaceship. Cyteronians can't exist on Earth in their natural form. The air is too thick here. The chemistry is wrong."

A faint bell rang somewhere in Summer's mind. She tried to locate it, but couldn't. "Then you put on a human form much like our astronauts put on a spacesuit."

"Kind of."

She looked at him again. "Who decides what you look like?"

"Me. I decided I wanted to look like the Marlboro Man. There he sits on his horse, looking positively rugged with his chaps and his Stetson and a cigarette in his hand."

"But you don't smoke."

"Would I dullen my sparkles?" he asked indignantly.

"And you don't look rugged. Well, maybe you do, but there's too much intelligence in your eyes for you to look like the Marlboro Man for long."

"Who do I look like?"

"You."

"Then I succeeded in fooling you."

"To some extent."

"What do you mean, to some extent?" he asked with spirit. "Admit it, Summer. I did fool you."

"No. I knew something was weird when you talked to me with your eyes. I actually heard those words."

"You didn't hear them, you felt them."

"I heard them. And then there was the way you could read my mind." She had a thought. "Why didn't you do it today? Why didn't you read my mind and come find me?"

"Because you didn't want to be found," he told her. "You wanted to sit scrunched up in those foolish mountain laurels at the edge of the meadow. If I'd gone out there and told you that the men weren't coming, you wouldn't have believed me. You thought I was nuts."

"Not nuts. Just different."

"Okay, different. Still I fooled you. Not once did you seriously think I might be an alien being."

He was right, of course. Even now, even with all he'd told her, she could stretch her imagination to believe that he'd made it up, in which case he was a man with a fertile fantasy life and a glib tongue.

Unsure which would be better for her, the alien or the dreamer, she extricated herself from his arms.

"Where are you going?" he asked.

"Just here." She went to the nightstand, took out the gun and hid it behind her back.

At the sight of it, Cameron sat straight up in bed. "What's that for?"

"How many bullets are in it?" she asked, wanting to test his powers.

"None. I took them out when I took the gun from your hand that first night. They're in the back of the drawer."

Thwarted, she dropped the gun on the bed. Her eyes skimmed the loft, finally pausing at the stereo cassette player on the shelf. She often let tapes put her to sleep.

Even now she could see a cassette in the slot. "What's in there? What was I listening to last?"

"Bach sonatas for harpsichord. I was listening to them myself today while I waited for you to come home."

"You're not making this easy," she complained.

"You're not asking the right questions," he countered. "Now if you were to ask me to *play* those Bach sonatas for harpsichord, I could accommodate you." He crossed his legs Indian-style, rested his hands palms up on his thighs, closed his eyes—and, albeit naked, looked so much like a meditating yogi that Summer nearly laughed aloud. But any sound that might have started to form in her throat was frozen there when she heard the unmistakable sound of the harpsichord—*her* harpsichord, the one downstairs in the corner of her living room—playing the very same sonata that was on the tape in her cassette player. The feeling of the music was different, the emotion more intense, but then, she wouldn't have expected anything less from Cameron.

She covered her face with her hands, and the playing instantly stopped. After a minute, she took a deep breath and dropped her arms to her sides. "Either you're playing a very cruel, very sophisticated game with me, or you really are an alien."

"Which do you think?" he asked.

With his eyes saying, *Trust me, I love you,* there was no real question in her mind. She supposed there hadn't been for a while. With the exception of the demise of his sailboat, most everything he'd ever told her was the truth. She did trust him. She did love him. And, God help her, she did believe that he loved her.

"I think," she said quietly, walking toward the bed, "that this isn't a game." She studied his face, touching each of his features with her eyes. When he held out a hand, she took it and let herself be drawn to his side. Settling her cheek on his chest, she gave a voluminous sigh.

"What is it, sweetie?" he asked with such tenderness that her throat grew tight.

She gave it a minute to ease, then spoke from the heart. "I don't want you to be an alien. I want you to be human like me. I want you to stay here forever."

He shifted his arms around her, pressing a kiss to the top of her head. In a voice that was muffled by her hair, he said, "I am human like you."

"Now. But there's a little white sparkle inside that'll take you over before long. You'll be lost to me then."

"No. Not if you don't want that."

"But you'll be *leaving*," she argued. Much as it hurt to think of that, she had to be a realist. He had said it himself; he was doing research, and Earth was only one of his stops. Someone, someday was going to want the results of his study, and for that, he'd have to return to Cyteron.

"You could leave with me."

"I can't. I'm human. *All* human."

For a minute he was silent. Then, in a tone of quiet conviction, he said, "No. You're not, Summer."

Her heart actually stopped. It tripped back into action seconds later, but only after she'd gone cold all over.

She drew away and stared at him. "What?"

"You're not . . . all . . . human."

Her mind buzzed. She cleared her throat. "I'm, uh, I was born here. So was my mother. So was her mother. And *her* mother."

"That's right. And her mother, your great-great-grandmother, was born on Cyteron."

Summer shook her head. "That can't be."

"Why not?"

"Because we're human." Before he could say another word, she rose from the bed and ran toward the stairs.

Cameron came right after her. "What are you doing?"

"Getting dressed," she said, almost falling down the stairs.

He was fast on her heels. "Why are you doing that? It's the middle of the night."

"I have to go out." She shut the bathroom door in his face.

"You can't go out," he yelled through the wood. "There's nowhere to *go* at this hour."

Grabbing clean clothes from the bathroom shelves, she hastily pulled them on. "I have to think."

"In that secret nook of yours?"

"You know about that, too?" she shouted, appalled. She hopped on one foot, nearly falling in her hurry to get her jeans on. "That's not fair!"

He opened the door. "Nothing's fair in love and war."

"You got it right," she murmured, but without looking at him. She angrily stuffed her shirttails into her jeans. "Maybe that problem wasn't for real, either."

"Hey, I thought we established that I really am an alien."

"You are. But not me." Putting her hands over her ears, she ran past him. "Don't say anything else, and *don't talk to my mind. I don't want to hear!*"

At the door, she pushed her feet into sneakers and grabbed her jacket from the hook. Then she ran from the cabin. She didn't know where she was going, only that she couldn't accept what he'd said. She was human, flesh and blood woman, and with each step deeper into the forest, she died a little more.

# 8

SUMMER WALKED FOR MILES through the predawn darkness. She took every out-of-the-way path on the island, moving briskly with her head down and her mind on all that had happened.

The events of that night alone were cause for trauma. First she'd nearly been raped, then she'd been made love to for the very first time. From the lowest of lows to the highest of highs, it was enough to shake even the steadiest of women, which Summer was, under normal circumstances. But the past week hadn't been a normal one for her by any measure, and the weekend even less so. The agony of loving Cameron and thinking that she would never see him again, then sitting for hours waiting for strangers to take over her meadow, had been pure hell.

Worst, *worst*, was the truth about Cameron. Cameron *Divine*. She shook her head at the irony of the name. No doubt he had chosen it with the same tongue-in-cheek humor with which he had chosen his looks. The Marlboro Man. Telling stories about her that were utterly impossible.

She walked on and on, never once fearing for her safety in spite of what Hallard Dunn had tried. Cameron was watching her. She knew it as surely as she knew that her name was Summer VanVorn and that she was entirely human. He would keep her safe. He did love her.

Her body tired long before her mind, though she kept walking. To sit still would be to feel the full force of her confusion, and it was bad enough without. Okay, she believed Cameron when he said that he was from an alien planet. It explained things she couldn't otherwise explain. But why was he saying that she was alien, too? That didn't make sense.

Was he hoping that she would accept him more if she thought she was like him? But she loved him already. She had told him that.

Was he hoping she would take to the baby more easily if she thought that the alien part of it was from her as well? But she would love the baby *any* way it came. Didn't Cameron know that?

Maybe there was something he wasn't telling her. Maybe the baby would come out looking grotesque. Maybe he wanted to prepare her for that. Or have her take part of the blame. But if that was so, why had he talked about a little boy with blond hair and blue eyes?

It didn't make sense at all.

As she grappled with the dilemma, the first light of dawn appeared on the eastern horizon. Without conscious thought, she crossed through the cornfield south of town and came out on a rutted path that ran behind a row of weathered cottages. She followed the path until she came to the cottage that belonged to Millie Osgood. Then, hands in her pockets, she took up position behind a large oak a safe distance away and waited.

Millie was an early riser. Summer knew that because she and the postmistress had often talked about the birds that came to feed in those early hours. Sure enough, before any of the neighbors had stirred from their homes, Millie came out the back door with a large bag of seed.

Stepping out from behind the tree, Summer watched her fill the tiered feeder that hung from her porch overhang. Summer wasn't sure why she had come here—perhaps because Millie was a friend and because Summer was desperately in need of one. But she didn't know what Millie could do for her. She certainly wouldn't have any more answers than Summer had herself.

Then again, maybe she would.

Millie looked up and caught sight of her. She broke into a smile that wreathed her face in sweet wrinkles, and with several short jerks of her hand waved Summer closer. By the time Summer reached the porch, Millie had the back door open. She shooed her inside, then gestured her into a seat at the small kitchen table.

Neither of them had yet said a word. Summer knew that Millie wouldn't want to broadcast the healer's presence to the neighbors, and for the first time, upset as she was, it bothered her. She wondered what it would be like to have real friends, to be able to walk in and out of someone else's home as so many of the islanders did, without needing either darkness or silence.

"There now," Millie said at last. She began to move around the kitchen in her slow, arthritic gait. "You'll have a cup of tea. Then you'll tell me what's wrong. You look like you haven't slept in days, Summer VanVorn."

At that moment, Summer felt as though she hadn't. She felt tired and sore, and that was only on the outside. Inside she hurt, too.

The tea was hot and beckoning. She wrapped her hands around the chipped cup and let the warmth seep into her fingers. She was thinking that her mother used to make tea as hot and beckoning, when Millie broke into the thought.

"Something happened down near the docks last night," she said nonchalantly as she stirred milk into her tea. "Hallard Dunn got beat up. There was a lot of rushing to clean him up before his wife got a look at him. Word was he was forcing himself on some pretty young thing when the boyfriend came along."

Summer shuddered. She raised questioning eyes to Millie's.

"Not that he was saying that, mind you. Kept his mouth shut tight as a drum. But his pants was undone. Looked from the way he was bending over like he'd been kicked in that area." Her faded eyes took on a twinkle. "Served him right, if you ask me. He's been trouble for years, and the whole town knows it. If he did force himself on a girl, it wouldn't have been the first time. Hallard Dunn is no good. No good. If you ask me, it'd be right nice if that kick damaged him permanently."

Summer's face drained of what little color it had. Had Cameron done that?

"Not that it did," Millie went on. "No-goods like Hallard always manage to come away with nothin' but scratches and bruises." She sipped her tea, then set the cup down. In a softer voice, she said, "Something's on your mind, Summer. Care to tell me what it is?"

Summer turned the cup in her hand. She raised it to her lips, took a small drink and lowered it to the saucer. *You shouldn't be here*, the tiny voice inside her said. *VanVorn women don't go to islanders for advice. They always take care of themselves*. But none of the Van-Vorn women had gone through what Summer was going through. At least, she didn't think they had.

Looking unsurely at Millie, she said, "You knew my mother. And my grandmother."

"Certainly did."

"As well as anyone else in town, would you say?"

Millie considered that for a minute. "I'd say."

"What do you remember about them?"

Again Millie took a minute. "They were pretty. Both of them. Had light hair like yours, and blue eyes." She frowned and corrected herself. "Your grandma had blue eyes. Your mama's were brown like yours."

*Blue eyes.* Summer swallowed. Blue eyes like Cameron's? Or blue eyes like millions of other human beings?

"And they were good-hearted," Millie went on. "Always had a smile for me, and some tea. Actually, from your grandma it was sweets. My daddy was the postmaster then, and I wasn't but a nuisance of a little thing playing under the counter when she came in. Sweets, she brought. Hard candies. Like the barley pops Ezra sells today, only better."

Summer remembered those candies. She hadn't ever had them herself, but her mother had talked of them often. Her grandmother had died before passing the recipe on, and no matter how many times her mother tried to make them—and she tried many, many times with many different ingredients, Summer recalled—she couldn't quite get them right. So Summer had had sweets, but not *those* sweets.

"They were smart, your mama and her mama were. Just like you are," Millie added.

But Summer didn't feel very smart. In fact, the more she thought about it, she felt perfectly *dumb*. There were so many questions. Why hadn't she asked them of her mother? Was it because life as Summer had known it had been good, so she'd had no cause to look deeper? Or because she lacked a certain curiosity? Or because her mother hadn't *wanted* her to ask?

Summer dropped her eyes to her tea. "They didn't come into town much, did they?"

"Say again?"

Summer looked up, remembered Millie's hearing problem, and repeated herself more clearly.

"They didn't mix any more than you," Millie answered, then chided, "but you know that."

"I know that my mother didn't, so I never did. Was my grandmother the same way?"

"Very much."

"And my great-grandmother?"

"Now, that was before my time."

"Did you hear stories about her?"

"Ah, yes."

"She was different from the rest right from the start?"

"So I hear."

"What else do you hear?" Summer asked. It wasn't exactly eagerness she felt, as much as desperation. She had to know more about those earliest VanVorns. "What do the stories say? Do they say anything about how VanVorns came to live on Pride, or about the first ones who did come?"

Millie's face grew more animated and at the same time distant. She looked as she had the week before in the post office, absorbed in the fictitious world of a book. "They say it happened during a storm," she began in a narrative way, "that the wind and the rain came and washed her right up onto the beach. They say that she knew her name—she must've been your great-great-grandmother, that one—but she didn't know much else about where she come from or who she was." Millie arched one sparse brow. "She wouldn't go into town. Wouldn't hear of that. No, right from the start, she knew she wanted to live in the woods. So they took here there, and the next time someone stopped to see how she was, she had the cabin built and all." The narrative tone ended. "That was when the stories started up."

"Just because she built the cabin herself?"

"How could a little thing like that build a cabin herself?" Millie replied indignantly. "Leastways they said she was a little thing, and from the looks of you and your mama I believe it."

"Maybe someone helped her," Summer suggested. There had to be a logical explanation for it. "Someone from town."

"In a day?" Millie shook her head. "It'd have to have been more like a *lot* of someones, and the word that came down said no. No one helped. She built it herself."

Summer took another tack. "Maybe it wasn't the cabin as we know it, but more like a lean-to. Even a small woman could put a lean-to together."

"No, it was the cabin. The same one you live in now. And that isn't all. They say she was growing things right after that, but no one knows where she got the seeds. They say she had money when she finally did come into town, but no one knows where she got it. They say she had *lots* of money, but when they found her washed up on shore, she had nothing."

Summer lifted a shoulder in a stab at a shrug. "Clearly someone gave her the money and the seeds. Maybe someone from the ship she was on, someone who washed up on shore right after she did."

Millie looked doubtful. "They say there was no one. They say she lived alone the whole time. There were some who took an interest in that, I hear."

Summer frowned. "I don't follow."

"They say she was a real beauty and that she had more than a few admirers in town."

Summer latched on to that. "See? An admirer must have built the cabin and given her money."

But Millie's reply came quickly, like the refrain of a song. "That's not what they say. They say that no one could get near her."

"What do you mean?"

"There was something around the cabin, something to protect her, something she put there that no one could get through. They couldn't see it, but they could only go so far and then no more. She could come and go. They couldn't."

"That's ridiculous," Summer scoffed. "People come to my cabin all the time when they want me. They used to come for my mother the same way."

"But not for that first one, your great-great-grandma. Maybe not for your great-grandma, either. By the time your grandma was doing the healing, the invisible whatever-it-was was gone."

Summer lifted her teacup and hid behind it for a minute. It rattled softly, betraying the unsteadiness of her hand, when she put it on the saucer. "If there ever was an invisible whatever, I'm sure it was only in the minds of the people who had already decided that there was something strange about her."

"Maybe," Millie admitted, then, caught by distant memory again, gave a soft sigh. "They still talk about her eyes, though. A dark, dark blue they were, near to navy. Hear tell, they'd look right at you and see *into* you. And then she started healing, and it seemed she *could* see into folks, leastways to know what to give them that'd make them better." Millie shivered. "Can't say as I blame folks for thinking her strange. It's not often you see eyes like that. I hear your young man's got them. Who is he, anyway?"

Very carefully, so as not to let her body shake on the outside the way it was on the inside, Summer dabbed her mouth with a small paper napkin, tucked the napkin under the edge of the saucer and rose from her chair. "He's a friend, someone I met while I was sailing. I have to go now, Millie. Thank you for the tea. It was just right."

Millie pushed herself up and followed Summer to the door. "You come again, now. I don't care what the rest of the town says, I think you're a very nice young woman. I'll root around in my head and try to find other stories about your relatives. It's too bad none of them kept any diaries. They would be such fun to read." She held the door open. "Now there's an interesting thought. Look through the cabin, Summer. Maybe one of them did write things down. If you find anything, you bring it to me to read to you, understand?"

Summer waved and jogged off. Under cover of the foliage on the far side of the rutted path, she ran in the direction of her woods. She skirted the cornfield this time and didn't slow until she was surrounded by the familiar pine scent. Even then her pace was brisk. She was breathing hard—from the exertion, from the upset, she suspected both—but she kept going until she reached a hillock not far from the cabin. There she dropped to her knees, then sat on her heels and, panting, looked at the small stone slabs that marked the graves of four generations of VanVorn women. None of the gravestones was etched. None needed to be. The only person who cared that they were there didn't need incomprehensible words to remind her who lay buried deep beneath the island soil.

"Oh, Mom," she whispered. She rocked back and forth, using the motion as a diversion from the pain she felt. "Is it true?"

A mourning dove cooed to its mate, while small creatures scampered along the forest floor.

Summer tangled her hands in the grass. "If you were alien, you'd answer me. You'd be able to speak from the grave. You'd be able to tell me *whether or not it's true*." She blew out a breath, then another one that came fast on its heels. Then she moaned, but not even that helped.

"It can't be," she decided. "It just can't be. I had a normal upbringing. There was nothing extraordinary or—or otherworldly about it. Okay, so I didn't go to school with the kids in town, but there's nothing so strange about that. I learned more than they did, and not by magic, but by hard work. You spent hours and hours reading to me. When I didn't understand things, you explained them. I didn't take any shortcuts. There *weren't* any." She paused. "Wouldn't there have been some if we'd had alien blood?"

A light breeze shushed through the pines.

"So I didn't have a father around. Lots of kids don't. So *you* didn't have one. It didn't matter. We had a nice life. We had a *normal* life. I had hamburgers and pizza and ice cream sundaes like the rest of the kids. We had a washer and a dryer, a food processor and a popcorn maker, and we were one of the first on the island to have a VCR. Okay, so we didn't have a car. We didn't *need* a car. There's nowhere to go to on Pride that required one. Besides, we had a whole band of ponies. If we couldn't get somewhere on foot, one of the ponies would have taken us."

She smiled wistfully, taken up with a picture from the past. "I always loved riding the ponies. Do you remember? When I was a little girl I used to beg you to put me on one. You'd tell me that they weren't made for taking riders, but that since I was small and light, if I was very gentle I could try it. Just for a minute, you said. Then you'd lift me up, and I'd be very, very gentle, and it was like I was floating. I loved that."

Her smile faded. She focused on her mother's grave. "Is it odd to love the ponies the way I do? Is there something alien about that? People do it all the time. Animal lovers. They communicate to their pets through the tones of their voices and the touch of their hands, and that's nothing different from what I do. There's no magic involved. It comes with caring."

Taking a deep breath, she dropped her head back and saw a patch of blue where the pine boughs above had parted. It was a beautiful day, just the kind when she and her mother would have taken baskets and gone berry picking. She remembered bringing the berries back, washing them, then standing away from the heat while her mother boiled them down into jelly. "Is there anything alien in that?" she cried. "Or in living alone? Or in using herbs to make people feel better?"

Once again she looked at the ground. "Tell me, Mom. Please?" But there was no response from the grave. Unable to help herself, she began to cry. "Is it true? Is it *true*? I need to know!"

There had been times in the last week when, being with Cameron then without him, she'd felt lonely. There had been times when she'd been confused about what she was feeling and had wished her mother had been there to explain. There were times when she'd been frightened—no, terrified. But at none of those times had she felt as starkly alone as she did now.

*Oh, Summer. Please, sweetie. Don't torment yourself so.*

The words penetrated her soft sobs. At first she thought it was her mother talking to her after all. Then she realized that the voice was Cameron's, and in the next instant she felt the strength of his arms enfolding her.

She wanted to shake him off, to tell him to leave her, to accuse him of entering her life and turning it upside down ten times over. But she needed him now. Maybe she always had. Maybe his coming to her had, in fact, been destined for years and years.

She raised her eyes to see him standing on the far side of the hillock. His hands were tucked in the pockets of his jeans, and his shoulders had a defeated slump to them that was so uncharacteristic as to shake her. Worse, though, was the look of uncertainty on his face. Not once had she seen quite as unsure a look. It struck her that she was its cause—and that she wanted it gone.

*I need you, Cameron,* she thought. *I need your help. Hold me now.*

The words had barely crossed her mind when he was moving toward her. Coming down on his knees, he took her in his arms and gathered her close. Her tears slowed. Her breathing steadied. She slid her arms around his waist and locked her hands at the small of his back.

"Why does it frighten you so," he asked, "the idea of having alien blood?"

She took a deep breath, but it was another minute before she had her thoughts together enough to answer him, and another minute yet that she spent listening to his heartbeat. It was certain, again. That gave her strength.

"All my life I've been different from other people—in small, subtle ways, but different nonetheless—and I always told myself that it didn't matter, that I was happy to be different, that I didn't need the acceptance or the friends. And I still do believe that. Only there's a small part of me that wishes it wasn't so, and that's the part that doesn't want to be any more different than I already am."

"You're not any more different. You're the same as you always were. It's just that now you have an explanation for those small, subtle differences you always felt."

"I'm not saying I buy the explanation," she said quickly.

"Sure you do. You're just wishing it wasn't so, and I can understand that, Summer, really I can. You've spent twenty-eight years thinking of yourself as one thing. To be suddenly told you're something else is bound to upset you."

She made a sound that said he should only know the half.

"But I don't," he returned candidly. "All I can do is feel what you're feeling now. I can't feel everything you've felt in the past. I can't know how the experiences you've had in life have affected your ability to take all this in. All I can do is to tell you it's not the end of the world. Just the opposite, in fact. Being alien—"

"*Part* alien," she cut in, then felt compelled to add, "if that."

He didn't pick up where he'd left off, but held her quietly for a minute. Pressing a gentle kiss to her forehead, he said, "Come on. Let's walk." He helped her up and took her hand.

Summer walked beside him, pausing before they rounded the hillock to cast a last look at her mother's grave. "Wouldn't she have talked to me just now if she'd been alien?"

"She's too far away to do that."

"She's too *dead* to do that."

"No. Too far away. She's on Cyteron."

Summer's step faltered. "She returned there when her human form died?"

"That's right."

"And she knew she was going?"

"At the end, yes."

For the sake of argument, Summer went along with him. "If my mother is on Cyteron, why are you on Earth? If your mission was to find out the effects of intermarriage on Cyteronians, why not simply ask the ones who've returned there? Why spend years traveling across the universe to get information that's available at home?"

"Because you're another generation. You're another dilution of Cyteronian blood. And because there's a value to observing you firsthand in the field."

"Then I'm a scientific experiment," she said and, with a sudden flare of anger, yanked her hand from his and stopped walking. "What gives you the right to toy with my life this way? I'm more human than Cyteronian."

"Then you do admit to having Cyteronian blood?"

"I admit to having *human* blood." But her anger quickly faded, and she murmured more quietly, "I don't even know if Cyteronians have blood."

Head down, she started walking again. Cameron was soon by her side. It was a full five minutes before he reached for her hand, and then she let him take it only because she felt chilled, and because his fingers were warm, and because touching that way was so very human.

Later, she wasn't sure whether she'd known where she was walking or whether it had been a purely subconscious thing, but somehow she wasn't surprised when they turned onto the path that led down to the beach where Cameron had carried her from the water on the day of the storm. The tide was out, offering a wider swath of sand to walk on than there had been then. Rather than walking now, though, they went to the water's edge.

Cameron brought her hand to his mouth, kissed its palm, then set it gently down by her side. Tucking his hands in the back waistband of his jeans, he faced the sea. "That day, when you were out there after your boat was destroyed, when you started to go under, just before I caught you, did you feel anything strange?"

"I felt panic," she said, remembering it all too well.

"Beyond that. Any sense of getting a second wind? Or of some unknown force inside you coming to life?"

She shook her head. "Only panic. Why?"

He dug a heel into the sand. "That's one of the things we've wondered about. We know that when someone like your mother is about to die, there's a distinct awareness of a new force rising to replace the old. That's Cyteronian energy taking over when the human energy fails. We don't know at what stage it takes over, though. Maybe you weren't close enough to death."

*Maybe I'm not a Cyteronian,* she thought. *Maybe you got the wrong girl.*

He sent her a plaintive look before dropping his gaze to focus on what his sneaker was doing. "The signs are all there, Summer. You can fight them and deny them and tell me that I've made a mistake, but if you stop to look at it fairly, you'll know I'm right."

She wanted to argue, to accuse him of using supernatural powers to twist her thoughts to his way of thinking, and she might have if he had been holding her hand, or touching her in some other way, or sending messages straight to her head. But he was standing apart from her with his eyes downcast. She was under no spell. She felt in full control of her own mind.

"I'm listening," she said softly, not because she wanted to but because she had to.

As though determined to give her that full control, he raised his eyes to the gently rolling waves. "There's the way you can feel a storm coming. Your body temperature rises, and your skin is sensitive to the touch. There's the way you play the pipe and the flute and the harpsichord. You can't read music any more than I can, yet you play it, and you hear much more than the notes. There's your healing ability." He held up a hand just as she opened her mouth to argue. "I know. You're thinking that most of what you do is good old-fashioned folk medicine, and that may be true, expect it only explains things to a point. Remember that fire at the Sulters' house several years back?"

"That was before my mother died," Summer said, wondering how he knew.

"Your mother was the one who told us about it. She was busy taking care of the father and you were left with the son. He was burned so badly that he'd never have lived through the night if you hadn't come, and it wasn't just the salve you put on his skin. It was your touch. Your heart nearly broke for the pain he was in."

But Summer was thinking of her mother. "'Concentrate on what you're doing,' she always told me. 'Focus your energy into mending what's broken and healing what's sick.'"

"That's right," Cameron said. "That's what we do."

"Did my mother know?"

"That she was using Cyteronian techniques? Probably not at the time. But she'd learned the technique from her mother, who had learned it from her mother before that."

"And my mother really told you about the Sulters' fire?"

"Not me. One of my colleagues, who then told me when I was preparing for this trip. How else would I know?"

Try as she might, she couldn't find another explanation for it. Tugging the sleeves of her sweater down to cover her hands, she said, "Go on. What other signs are there that I'm part Cyteronian?"

"The way you think things into happening."

"I don't. I *can't.*"

"You filled the meadow with snakes, then bugs, then puddles."

"That wasn't me."

"There's no one else here who could *begin* to do any of those things, and they weren't flukes of nature, Summer. You thought all those things into being, just like I thought the Mundys into coughing and Jeb Strunk into falling and your harpsichord into playing Bach sonatas. You have the power."

"I *don't.* I wish I did, believe me, there are times I wish it. But it just doesn't work."

"It works," he said so simply that she looked at him. He met her gaze for several seconds before returning his own to the sea. "It works, though maybe not as quickly or consistently as it did with your mother or grandmother. You said it yourself. With each generation, each crossbreeding, the power becomes less intense. Combine that with your loss of confidence in it, and the results are definitely diluted."

"I still think you're wrong," she said, but more meekly, because if indeed it was possible for an alien to live and mate with humans, what Cameron was saying made sense.

"It's interesting," he mused. "When you tell yourself that you can't do things, you can't. Right now, if I were to ask you to drag the ocean floor for a piece of debris from your sailboat, you wouldn't be able to do it, because you have yourself convinced that you can't. But if something made you angry enough to forget your supposed limitations, you'd be able to do whatever you wanted. That was what happened the time after your mother died, when you were nearly raped."

"What do you mean?" Summer asked, feeling an odd premonition.

"You hated the man who'd done it. You wished him dead. And then he was."

"That was an accident," she said quickly. When Cameron only continued to stare at the waves, she asked a bit frantically, "I'm a *murderer* then?"

His eyes shot to hers. "Of course not. There was no intent involved. He got what was coming to him."

She shivered. Curling her hands into fists inside the cuffs of her sweater, she folded her arms under her breasts. "What about the men who did impregnate VanVorn women? Where did they come from?"

"Just where each said. They were human."

"Was it coincidence, each one's coming here for just one night?"

Cameron slowly shook his head.

"Don't stop now," she said facetiously when he didn't hurry on.

"Those men were hand chosen. They were picked for their looks, their brains and their physical dexterity."

"*We* picked them?" She wondered if the earlier VanVorn women had powers she hadn't begun to imagine.

But Cameron said, "No. *We* did. There are Cyteronians who specialize in picking mates."

"Matchmakers," Summer said and wanted to laugh. The story was getting more and more complex, and the worst of it was she couldn't discount any part. Nor could she stop asking questions. "How did they get here?"

"They were more or less led. A bug put in their rear, so to speak."

She winced. "Not in their rear. In their ear."

He smirked. "It makes more sense my way."

"Cameron."

He relented. "All of them had been adventurers to some extent, so it wasn't hard."

"Did they know why they were here?"

"The real reason? No. But they legitimately fell in love with VanVorn women."

"If that was so, why didn't they come back?"

"We didn't want them to, so we cleared their minds of the women and the love."

Knowing after the weekend just past what it meant to love and live without, Summer said, "That was cruel."

"True, but it would have been more cruel for those men to come back and take our women from Pride. They weren't meant to live on the mainland. They needed a simpler life." He frowned and looked at the sand. "Things here weren't ideal. We knew about the scorn you all have had to endure. But there was healing to be done. And there were the ponies to care for."

Something about the way he said it gave Summer a second premonition, this one less ominous than the first, indeed exciting. "What about the ponies?" she asked.

Cameron gave her a crooked smile, the kind that never failed to send warm little tingles up and down her spine. "You tell me."

"They're from Cyteron?" When he nodded, she said, "Then the beech trees here really are different from beech trees elsewhere?" When he nodded again, she asked, "Where do the ponies go each winter?" He gave her a knowing look. "Cyteron?" she cried. "You're kidding!" He shook his head. "Then the bunkenberry bushes are on Cyteron," she concluded with a laugh, recalling what he'd told the selectmen, "where the altitude is higher, the air thinner and the soil composition totally different. Those poor guys are probably asking all over if anyone has ever heard of bunkenberry bushes." She laughed again, feeling the warmth of a joke shared with Cameron, until she realized the implication of it. Uneasy again, she gazed along the beach.

As though he, too, realized the implication of the sharing, he spoke more intimately. "When we first met, you thought I looked familiar. That was the Cyteronian element, Summer. Your eyes may not be blue like mine, but there's something behind the lenses—hard to find a human word to describe it because it's almost intangible, but you saw it. When you looked at me, you saw something you'd seen in yourself and in your mother."

She pursed her lips toward the sand.

"And then," he concluded even more gently, "there's the matter of our problems."

Her head came up. "What problems?"

"Mine is confusing idioms. Since they don't always make perfect sense word for word, I have trouble getting them straight, especially when I'm upset or distracted. Your problem is reading."

She tipped up her chin. "It's not a problem."

"You can't do it."

"Yes, I can."

"Not really. You know your name and simple words, but putting them together is a problem."

"It isn't."

"Then why don't you ever read books?"

"Because I choose not to."

"Why is that?"

"Because there's no *need* to read. I listen to tapes and I watch television." She scowled. "Don't look at me that way, Cameron. Just because I choose not to read doesn't mean I can't."

He studied her for another minute before giving a nod. "Okay. Let's see you do it."

Horrified, she watched him drop to his haunches and start drawing letters in the sand. She recognized her name, simply because she was so familiar with it, and she caught the words *I, to* and *a,* but she was struggling with the rest when he sat back on his heels, where he stayed for what had to be the longest moments of Summer's life. To his credit, he didn't look at her. She would have died if he had. As it was, the humiliation she felt was devastating.

"Now try this," he said. Scooting to a fresh patch of sand, he drew a new set of letters.

Summer's heart beat an increasingly rapid tattoo as she watched the new words form in the sand. She put a sweater-covered fist to her mouth and held it there until, once again, he sat back on his heels.

"Well?" he asked, raising expectant eyes to hers.

Her hand slid to steady her heart. In a soft, disbelieving but enchanted voice, she read, "'Shall I compare thee to a summer's day? Thou art more lovely and more temperate.' That's Shakespeare. My mother used to read me the sonnets when I lay in bed at night." She couldn't take her eyes from the words. "What did you do?" she asked excitedly. "How did you change it?" She looked at the first message, which was as jumbled as before, then at the second, which remained crystal clear. "Do they say the same things?"

"Word for word."

"But I can read this one." And with such ease! She couldn't believe it!

Cameron rose and brushed sand off his knees. "That's because I've written it in characters that make sense to the Cyteronian part of our brain. It's a problem we've come across often with our people on Earth. It wasn't so bad in the old days when education here was more lax. If a person read, fine. If he didn't, there was always something else that he could do. Then the schools started focusing on learning disabilities, and our problems became more noticeable."

"Write something else," Summer ordered eagerly. "Something else I can read."

Moving several feet from his original message, Cameron squatted and wrote, "Roses are red, violets are blue, sugar is sweet and so is glue."

She laughed in delight. "Something else."

"My finger's getting tired."

"Something short."

With an indulgent smile, he found a clean spot of sand and in large clear letters wrote, "*Je t'aime.*"

She threw her arms around his neck, fearing that if she didn't ground herself she would float right up into the air, she felt that buoyant and light. "I thought I was dumb."

"You're not dumb," he assured her, coming to his feet. "You're Cyteronian."

"All these years I thought there was something wrong with me. My mother didn't have this problem."

"Not all of us do. I don't. Your mother didn't. You do. It has something to do with the way genes mix at the time of conception. Kind of like eye color. It's very possible that our son will be able to read perfectly."

Summer had an awful thought. "What if he can't?"

"If he can't, he'll do just what you've done."

"But that's not good enough. If your civilization is so advanced, surely it knows how to repair the problem."

Cameron shook his head. "Not yet. We have computers that can take this—" he pointed to the first lines he'd written "—and transform it into this." He pointed to the words she could read. "But we don't know how to repair the problem in here." He pointed to his head.

That saddened her. "You have no idea how inadequate I've always felt. I wouldn't want my son to experience that."

Cameron draped an arm over her shoulder. "If he's living on Cyteron, it won't be a problem."

*Living on Cyteron?* Who said anything about living on Cyteron? Breaking from his hold, she started backing away. "Oh, no. I won't let you do that, Cameron. A child needs his mother. You can't take him away from me. I won't let him go."

Cameron was frowning at her. "Take him away from you? Why would I want to do that?"

"So he'd be with you on Cyteron."

He looked confused, then disbelieving, then pained. "With me? With you, too! Land's sake, Summer, why do you think I've been telling you all this about who you are and how you came to be here? It's part of the reclamation process. I'm taking you back with me. Didn't you guess?"

# 9

*I'M TAKING YOU BACK with me. Didn't you guess?*

Summer was stunned. Drawing her hands inside the cuffs of her sweater again, she hugged herself to ward off a sense of impending upheaval as she mutely shook her head.

"Well, I am," Cameron insisted belligerently. His feet were planted firmly in the sand, his square jaw set. "It wasn't in the original game plan, but that's how things work sometimes. They wanted me to come here and observe, that's all, observe. Then you nearly drowned and I had to swim you to shore, then you were all battered and I had to make you better, and by that time I had a feeling I was in trouble, because each time I looked at you, I wanted to keep on looking, and now that we've made love, there's no choice at all. I'm not letting you go, Summer. You're coming back with me."

His conviction struck a note of raw terror in her. She had a vision of her life disintegrating in a tragic scientific mistake. "I can't go," she cried. "I'm human. I can't go where little sparkles of white go."

"You can if you want."

"But I'm *human*."

"Only part."

She would have fought him on that, insisting that his story was too bizarre to believe, except that it wasn't. He had made his argument so conclusively that it would have been a waste of breath to try to repudiate it. As

strange as the thought was, she had to admit that she did
have Cyteronian roots. "But part human is enough to
keep me on Earth," she contended. "You said it, too—
with each new generation of cross-breeding comes a dilution of ability."

"Caused primarily," he put in, "by a loss of faith.
When pull comes to push, you can do whatever you
want."

*When push comes to shove,* she thought distractedly.

"Same difference," he said. "Your mother had faith.
That was what got her off Earth when her time here was
done."

Summer's heart skipped a beat. What she would give
to see her mother again! She made a small sound of
wanting, but it was lost to more practical considera-
tions. She glanced at herself. "I couldn't travel like this,
could I?" They both knew she wasn't talking about her
clothes.

He shook his head.

"Only sparkles travel?"

"In our ships."

"Could I really become a sparkle?"

"If you wanted."

"And I'd leave here forever?"

He nodded.

The fear returned. "But I've lived here all my life."

*So?* his raised brows asked.

She glanced behind her, where the granite boulders
were solid and steadying. Above them were scrub pines,
and around those, beach grass, all familiar and safe. "So
I can't leave. I've never been comfortable anywhere else."

Cameron folded his arms on his chest. "That's because you thought you were different from other people. You thought you wouldn't fit in. You thought that if

you couldn't read, you couldn't function, and that if you couldn't function, you'd be lost. But there's a good reason you're different from other people, and that's because you're Cyteronian. On Cyteron, you'd fit right in."

"No, I wouldn't," she argued in dismay. "I'd be different from them because of my human part. I'd be as much an outsider there as I am here."

"Uh-uh. The Cyteronian part is stronger. It's extraordinarily regenerative, far more so than the human part. By the time we passed through six galaxies, you'd be Cyteronian through and through."

She couldn't conceive of passing through one galaxy, let alone six. Her life on Pride had been good. She had the warmth of her cabin, the fruitfulness of her garden, the reward of treating the sick, even the occasional pleasure of talking with Millie. And she had the meadow. "I can't leave the ponies. They may be here for only three months out of the year, but they need me."

"We'll send someone else to tend them."

For every solution he had, she had another worry. "But I wouldn't know what to *do* there!"

His face softened. "You'd be with me. Wouldn't that be enough?"

She didn't have an answer for him. When she tried to picture Cyteron, she came up with a featureless void. She couldn't imagine what the place looked like any more than she could imagine what *she* would look like if she was there. She had no idea what its daily life was like, whether Cyteronians ate food as humans did, worked, slept or played as humans did. She had no idea what Cameron would look like on Cyteron, or what it would be like to be with him there. As always, the softening of his features now touched her deep inside, but she had no idea whether that softening and its effect had a counterpoint on Cyteron.

There were only two things she did know. The first was that she loved Cameron in his earthly form. The second was that the future frightened her.

Unfolding his arms, Cameron approached her. "Too much at once?" he asked and gently touched her cheek.

She nodded.

"We'll give it time, then." He slipped a firm, familiar arm around her shoulders and started walking her down the beach. "There's no rush. I'm not expected back for a while."

"WHAT'S IT LIKE THERE?" Summer asked. She had been asleep for most of the afternoon in the meadow, helpless to fight it since she hadn't slept a wink the night before. She was holding Cameron's hand, alternately lying beside him, half over him, or with her head on his thigh as she was now. He was her first thought when she opened her eyes. Cyteron was her second thought.

"It's bright," he said. "It's pleasant and cheerful."

"Is there grass?"

"Sure. And trees. And flowers. But they're different from yours. They're smaller and more delicate. *We're* smaller and more delicate."

"You really are just little sparkles?"

He gave her a pinch. "There's nothing 'just' about us. We're complex beings, each one of us different from the next."

"Like snowflakes?"

"Exactly."

"But you don't melt."

"Nope. We last and last."

"Forever?" It was an intriguing thought, being able to stay with Cameron until the end of time. Of course, she was still picturing him in his Marlboro Man body, and that wasn't the one that would last.

"Not forever," he said. "Even Cyteronians peter out after a while."

"How long a while?"

"A few hundred years."

She gasped. "Like vampires."

"Not like vampires," he scolded. "We're very much alive and happy. We get better as we get older."

She looked at him. "How old are you now?"

"In Earth years, in my nineties. In Cyteron years, in my thirties. It takes us three times as long to circle our sun, hence our years are three times as long. That life span I gave you was in Cyteron years."

Which meant that a Cyteronian life span was the equivalent of six hundred Earth years. It boggled her mind. "How do you *do* it?" she asked in awe.

"The secret is in the life form. Physiologically speaking, we're smaller, simpler and more efficient than humans, so we don't suffer the same wear and tear. We're better built, so we last longer. We're also happier, and happiness is an important element in longevity. Even here, that's the case. An unhappy person is more prone to accident and disease."

"Why are Cyteronians happier?"

"For starters, because there isn't the strife on Cyteron that there is on Earth. We don't have poverty. We don't have famine. We don't have war."

"Do you live in cities?"

"No, nothing as big as that. We live in small hamlets."

"How are you governed?"

"We have a representative form of government, but it's more a managerial body than anything else. We're a peaceful people."

"No fights? No competitive edge? No dissension?" Given what she regularly saw on the news, she couldn't imagine it.

"There isn't any cause for any of those things. We're healthy and prosperous. There's plenty to go around."

"But inevitably some have more than others, and then there's trouble."

"Not on Cyteron. We're far more a cerebral society than a physical one. Having wealth, *owning* things, just isn't valued. That's one of the reasons we put our people on Earth in places like Pride. The simplicity of the island simulates life at home."

"But I do own things," Summer pointed out. "And I am wealthy." Thought of that made her frown. "You once asked me where the money originally came from. Do *you* know?"

"No. That was one bit of information I wasn't given. My guess," he said with a twinkle in his eye, "is that your great-great-grandmother lifted it."

"*Stole* it?"

"Graciously, of course. Either that, or counterfeited it."

"She wouldn't have," Summer said.

"How else would she get it?"

"How did you get it?"

"Through a bank card. Things are easier for us now that you folks have become computerized. One central deposit can fund any number of us."

He hadn't said exactly where the money for that one central deposit had come from, but Summer wasn't sure she wanted to know, any more than she wanted to think of her great-great-grandmother as a crook.

"On occasion," Cameron said, reading her mind, "our people have to do certain things to guarantee their survival that they might not otherwise choose to do. She needed a nest egg to get her going, so she created it whatever way she could." His mouth thinned. "If she was paid as well for her work as Morgan Shutter paid you the other night, I'd say that nest egg was earned several times over."

Summer heard his sarcasm. "That still bothers you, doesn't it?"

"That Shutter didn't pay you? It sure does."

"But you just said that Cyteronians aren't driven by the need for wealth or possessions."

"We're not. We're driven by the need for common decency. It wasn't the money that bothered me, it was the lack of gratitude. You'll never find that at home."

His use of the future tense prompted her to remind him, "I didn't say I was going."

"You'll go."

"Go on," Cameron coaxed. "Try it."

Summer eyed the crushed soda can that lay on the fence post. Several inches of air separated it from the trash can from which he'd taken it. A good, stiff breeze might have easily returned it there, but there wasn't any breeze, let alone a stiff one, which was going to make Summer's point. Without nature's help, she was totally incapable of moving that can.

It was a hot and humid Wednesday. Having spent the morning putting up tomatoes and corn, she and Cameron were walking into town for the mail and supplies. The trash can in question was by the roadside at the third of the small houses they'd encountered. There was no one in sight.

Cameron stood casually by her shoulder, his head lowered, his mouth not far from her ear. "Concentrate," he said softly. "Clear your mind of everything but that soda can and the trash bin. Think the can up and off the fence."

But Summer could only think about the western movies she'd seen where the fledgling cowboy propped a can on a fence and took shaky aim. "I need my gun," she mused.

"Concentrate."

She stared at the can. "This won't work."

"That's your human side speaking. Listen to the Cyteronian part. It's telling you you can do it."

"I can't hear it."

"That's because you keep talking. Shut up and concentrate."

She continued to stare at the can. "Y'know, they missed something when they taught you English. 'Shut up' is not a polite way to speak to someone, especially someone you claim to love."

"Concentrate, Summer."

"I *am*."

"Clear your mind."

"It's clear."

"Think about the can."

"I'm thinking about it."

"Let your mind lift it."

She thought about all the horror flicks she'd seen in which strange forces moved things from one spot to another, but nothing happened to her can. "See?" She looked at Cameron. "I'm powerless."

He scowled at her. "You're your own first enemy."

"Worst enemy."

"You got *that* right."

"Okay," she said, "*you* move the can."

He shot a dark look at the fence post, where the soda can skipped neatly into the trash bin, then he took her hand and started off. "You have to want to do it, Summer."

"I do."

"You don't. You're afraid of it. You're afraid of the ramifications of it. You don't want to prove that you have the power, because you're afraid of leaving Earth."

"Well, wouldn't you be?" she asked. "If you'd spent your entire life here thinking of yourself as human, wouldn't you be afraid of suddenly taking another form, leaving everything that's near and dear and flying off to a totally foreign place?"

"It's not totally foreign. It's as familiar to you as that look in your eyes. I'm telling you, Summer, Cyteron is a fabulous place."

"Fine for you to say," she murmured. "It's your home. What if I don't like it?"

"You'll like it."

"But what if I don't? Can I take the next plane back here?"

"Sorry, sweetie, but we don't run regular shuttles across the universe. Maybe in another thousand years, but neither of us will be around to see that. Our grandchildren might."

She held his hand tighter. Whenever he mentioned their children, or in this case their grandchildren, she felt a stirring inside. She could have sworn he was able to reach in and caress her womb, for the need that was building there was making the thought of remaining on Earth without Cameron harder and harder to bear.

"Hey," he suddenly said with a grin as he drew her up short. "Look at that puppy."

She followed his gaze to where the Pinkneys' mongrel pup was playing with a small rubber ball.

"Let's have some fun," Cameron said, and before Summer had a chance to ask what he had in mind, the ball skittered away from the puppy, which bounded joyfully in pursuit, only to have the ball skitter away again just before the moment of capture. The puppy crouched down on its front paws with its tail in the air, then leaped after the ball, only to catch it, drop it and watch it lob off in another direction.

"Poor thing," she said, but in the next instant she was laughing. The puppy seemed to be having the time of its life.

"You try it," Cameron suggested, moving very close to her again. "Clear your mind. Concentrate on the ball. Think it up and away from the pup."

But Summer was thinking that she loved it when Cameron was close to her. She loved the size of his body, its scent, its virility. She leaned back an inch to bring their bodies into contact.

The puppy was in its crouched position again, tail wagging in anticipation, but the ball didn't move.

"Think it up," Cameron whispered by her ear.

She turned her head his way, putting his mouth by her cheek. "There's only one thing I can think up when you're this close to me."

He moaned and straightened. She didn't move.

"Well, it worked." He sighed.

She dared a glance behind and down. "So it did," she said with a satisfied smile and looked forward again. If nothing else, she mused, she had some power, and Cameron had been the one to awaken her to it. They had made love the night before and again at dawn. Each time was better than the last.

"Clear your mind," Cameron ordered gruffly.

"Let's leave that poor dog alone."

"Fine, but we can't move on until you clear your mind. Come on, Summer. This is embarrassing."

*That cumbersome human getup giving you trouble?* she asked, but she turned her eyes forward, toward town.

*Damn straight,* came the thought from behind her. *It's hard to control.*

*Is there an equivalent to it on Cyteron?*

*Oh, yeah. But it's not as obvious. Let me tell you, relative to the men on this planet, women have it easy.*

*Easy?* she echoed in good-humored dismay. *Our reproductive systems are far more troublesome than yours. We have to put up with PMS and cramps, then childbirth, which is no laughing matter.*

*Says the voice of experience.*

*Give me nine months and it'll be so.*

*Make that six months, Cyteronian time.*

*Eighteen months to grow a baby?* she cried. *Why so long?*

*We like being pregnant, so we prolong the pleasure. In the case of you and me, it'll give us a chance to be alone together before the baby comes.*

Summer took a deep breath and started walking again. When Cameron fell into step beside her, she said, "We could have nine months alone together if you stayed here. Why can't you do that, Cameron?" It seemed a viable alternative to her, one that would certainly be less threatening.

"Because I'm expected back," he said, "and besides, intergalactic travel, with a change in life form, is tricky with a newborn. I won't take that risk."

She turned to him, walking sideways now. "Then let's stay here. Let's have the baby and stay here until he's old enough to travel. That'd be fair—half his life on Earth, half on Cyteron."

"Could be a problem for me," Cameron said.

"How?"

"I'm a research scientist. I've traveled a lot, which means that I've taken more than one form that isn't natural to my composition. I can't remain human for long or I'll have trouble switching back. It's what you'd call an occupational hazard."

"Then stay here forever," she urged.

But he shook his head. "I'd be dead within a year. I need the chemistry of Cyteron." His eyes sharpened on the road ahead. "Uh-oh. Looks like we were expected."

Emerging from the inn were Hapgood Pauling, Keegan Benhue and Oaker Dunn. They came down the walk as a threesome and turned onto the road the same way. They looked as if they meant business.

Cameron's voice dropped to a theatrical murmur. "It's a scene straight out of *Gunfight at the OK Corral*, only none of them looks like Kirk Douglas."

Summer gave a nervous chuckle. "That's an understatement. For the life of me, I don't know why they button their shirts right up to the throat that way."

Suddenly Keegan's top button popped off. Startled, he reached up and touched the spot where it had been seconds before.

"You did that," Cameron accused in a whisper.

"I didn't," she whispered back. "You must have."

"No way. If I'd done anything, it'd be to trip Oaker. Looks like he's soused." As though on cue, Oaker stumbled. He caught his balance and turned in circles searching the road for what might have tripped him.

"Stop that," Summer chided under her breath, then turned a polite smile on the three. "Hapgood. Keegan. Oaker."

"Summah," Keegan said, stopping a good ten feet away and looking wary even then. "We were just coming to see you. Now that you're here in town, you've saved us the trip."

"How can I help you?"

Keegan cast an uneasy glance at Cameron, who, with his legs planted wide and his hands low on his hips, appeared ready to draw his six-shooter at the blink of an eye. When Keegan looked at Summer, he was paler than before. "You got to leave Pride for a bit," he said. "The folks from OSAY is stirring up some trouble."

"What kind of trouble?" Cameron asked.

Hapgood answered. "Seems that someone told 'em Pride was haunted."

"You told 'em," Oaker said.

Keegan scowled and hushed him before turning to Summer again. "We ain't got no proof about nothing, but they was scared off from coming to look at your meadow. Now it seems one of them told his cousin, who works for *People* magazine, and the cousin is coming up here to look for himself and write about what he sees."

"This fella called Keegan on the phone," Hapgood put in. "Said he heard there was a witch here. Keegan said there wasn't no witch, but this fella says he's coming to see."

Keegan held up a hand to still Hapgood so he could speak himself. "Fact is that if he comes here and talks with you and gets an idea that some of what his cousin was sayin' might be true, he's gonna write a big piece, and after that there'll be no chance in hell that anyone's ever gonna want to come up here to develop that land."

"So much the better," Summer said. "I've been telling you for years that the meadow shouldn't be developed."

Oaker shook a finger at her. "Y'*are* a witch. They won't say so in as many words, but y'*are*." He grunted when Keegan swatted him in the stomach with the back of his hand.

Hapgood took that opportunity to say, "What you are or aren't don't much matter t'us. All's matters is Pride. You know our reason for not wanting that fella to write about us. Way we see it, you got reason not to want him to come, too."

"What's that?" she asked.

Keegan resumed. "If he writes about that meadow bein' haunted, he's gonna write about you doin' it, and if he does that, you'll have people comin' up here just to stare at you. You'll be a spectacle. A curiosity. Don't know how you'd take to that, living quiet and alone like you usually do." He spared Cameron another look, then said, "Now, we was just meetin' at the inn and it hit us that that wouldn't be bad for us a'tall, not a'tall. Tourists start comin' up here and we stand to make money. 'Course, us bein' a private kind of island, we'd rather have something smaller and steadier and more upright than that." He shrugged. "But it's up to you."

*People coming up here just to stare?* she thought, appalled. *He's right. I'd hate that. Do you think he's bluffing?*

*Hard to tell.*

*Maybe he's just trying to get me off the island so they can bring another group in to see the meadow.*

When Cameron didn't answer her, she looked at him. He was studying the selectmen, hooded eyes going from one face to the next. After a moment's silence, he started forward. His steps were slow, broad and confident.

*This isn't the OK Corral,* Summer warned, worried he'd put a dimple in his chin and effect a Kirk Douglas drawl.

*Have faith, sweetie,* he said. *Have faith.*

She did have faith, she realized. Knowing about Cameron and where he was from, she knew that he wouldn't have the ponies harmed. So she remained where she was.

He came to a halt directly before the trio. "Gentlemen," he began in a deep voice, "Miss VanVorn appreciates your concern for her well-being, if indeed it is genuine. Frankly, we're not sure if it is. It occurs to us that you may have very different reasons for wanting her off Pride, even if only for a few days."

"We don't," Keegan protested with wide eyes.

Summer wasn't sure whether it was intimidation or honest indignation that she saw there. In either case, she remained silent while Cameron went on.

"When is this writer due here?" he asked.

"Friday morning," Keegan answered.

"What's his name?"

"Jonathan Brigham."

*One of the OSAY men was named Noah Brigham,* Cameron told Summer. *This could be legit.* "If I call the magazine, will they know who he is?" he asked Keegan.

"If they don't, then he's a fraud," Keegan blustered.

"How long will he be here?"

"He's stayin' at the inn Friday night. Should be gone by sundown Saturday."

Cameron straightened his shoulders. "Friday and Saturday. If Miss VanVorn does go somewhere for those days, will she return to find that you've sold the meadow to the owner of a spaghetti emporium?"

"*Spaghetti* emporium," Oaker spat out. "Why'd we ever want a spaghetti emporium?"

Cameron kept his eyes on Keegan. "Or a resort or a real estate development or a chocolate factory?"

"I swear," Keegan said, raising a hand, "we got no plans for anything like that, leastways not this weekend. You truly think we could'a got someone else interested in coming here so soon after you soured it with the satellite people?"

He had a point, Summer realized.

"No, I don't suppose you could," Cameron said, "and that's good, because if she does find that anything like that's been done in her absence, I can't guarantee what'll happen."

"Whaddya mean?" Oaker growled.

Cameron looked at him. "You've got a new pickup truck that you paid a bundle for? Make a deal for the meadow, and that pickup truck, or any other vehicles you try to drive, will stall over and over again, but only for you." He looked at Keegan. "Make a deal for that meadow, and the termites that are eating at your next-door neighbor's house will turn to yours." He looked at Hapgood. "Make a deal for that meadow, and your wife's hair will turn green." He frowned and stepped back. "Do I make myself clear, gentlemen?"

Oaker turned to Keegan and whined, "Who's he to talk t'us like that?" But Keegan only grabbed his arm and started him toward the inn.

Cameron returned to Summer's side. "Did I make myself clear?"

"Very. But I'm not going away."

He took her hand. "Come on. Let's get some lunch."

"I'm not going away, Cameron."

He didn't answer, but walked on wearing a broadening smile.

"I'm *not*," she insisted. "Why are you grinning that way?"

"Because I got the greatest idea while I was talking with them, and the more I think about it the greater it sounds. Let's go to New York."

Pulling her hand from his, she stopped walking. "New York? I'd *die* in New York."

He faced her, put both hands on her shoulders, then ducked his head to her level for emphasis. "No, you wouldn't. You'd be with me. Listen," he said with an eagerness that appealed to her even when his words didn't, "New York is one of the wonders of the modern world, yet neither of us has ever been there. Now, that's pathetic. How can we possibly return to Cyteron without having seen it? I mean, that'd be like visiting Arizona without seeing the Grand Canyon, or visiting Egypt without seeing the pyramids, or visiting Las Vegas without seeing a casino. You don't go to Earth without seeing New York," he said with finality.

"*You* see New York. I'm staying here."

"But I want to see it with you. That's what New York's about—two people together in the middle of the hustle and bustle. New York is interesting. It's exciting. It's romantic."

"It's also dirty."

"So we'll take a suite at the Plaza and we'll go in the Jacuzzi three times a day. Come on, sweetie, it'll be such fun."

She closed her eyes against the enthusiasm in his, but that didn't stop him.

"We could walk up and down Fifth Avenue, go to the top of the Empire State Building, see the Rockettes at

Radio City." He was clearly getting into it. "We could take a stroll through the park, or ride in a horse-drawn carriage. We could eat at Lutece or La Cirque, go to movies or the theater or visit museums, and if we didn't want to do any of that, we could stay in our suite, order a lavish dinner from room service and make love between each course." He took her face in his hands and whispered, "That's what I want, to make love to you on a window seat overlooking Central Park. Would that ever be an incredible experience!" His eyes soothed her like velvet. "You wouldn't have to be frightened, because I'd be there taking care of you all the way. Come on, Summer. What do you say?"

She squeezed her eyes shut this time. "Too expensive."

"Money's no problem. I have an unlimited expense account."

Her eyes came open fast. "You'd call this a *business* expense?"

"Business, pleasure," he mocked, "it's all the same on these intergalactic junkets." With a delighted laugh, he hauled her into his arms. "This is a great idea! Look at it as our swan song. Our last fling on Earth." He caught in a breath, held her again and leveled her an earnest stare. "Our honeymoon."

"We're not married."

"We can do it there. Wouldn't *that* be something to tell our grandkids some day."

"Cameron, you're impossible," she cried and it was true. He was impossible to resist. It struck her that she hadn't known life could be so full until she'd met him.

"You'll go with me?"

"To New York," she specified. She still wasn't comfortable committing herself to Cyteron. Perhaps she would be able to come to terms with it over the weekend. "But if we get hopelessly lost in that concrete jungle, it'll be your fault. If we get mugged, it'll be your fault."

"You're going to love it, Summer. Confess. You've always wanted to go there."

"I've always wanted to go there," she confessed because he was right. New York intrigued her, but she would never have dared go alone. With Cameron guiding her and keeping her safe, the idea appealed to her a lot. "But I want you to promise nothing will happen in the meadow while we're gone. I want you to *promise*. And I'll hold you to your word."

"I promise," he said solemnly, but the solemnity barely had time to settle before he broke into a beatific grin. In its light, Summer felt blessed.

## 10

WHEN CAMERON DID NEW YORK, he did it in style. Summer hadn't quite expected that, though in truth she hadn't given much thought to the way they would do things. Her focus was on leaving Pride, and the guilt and worry she felt about that. Once aboard Thursday's midday ferry to the mainland, her thoughts turned to surviving the flight from Portland and, even more daunting perhaps, given all she'd heard on the subject, the taxi ride from LaGuardia into the city.

They carried a single backpack between them. Summer had assumed they would wander around New York wearing the same jeans they wore on Pride, but Cameron had other ideas. The first thing he did upon their arrival in the city was to usher her into Saks Fifth Avenue, where he proceeded to outfit them both for the weekend.

"This is absurd," Summer protested in a stage whisper when she emerged from the dressing room wearing a short, chic chemise whose price tag she had just taken a look at.

"It is not," he whispered back. He was smiling broadly, thoroughly enjoying the show through sparkling navy eyes.

Summer edged closer to him so that the saleswoman wouldn't hear her. "But we'll never wear these things again." There was no cause whatsoever to wear silk dresses on Pride. "It's *obscene* to spend so much money for one or two wearings."

"All the better," he said, turning her so that he could have a rear view. "Obscenity is an Earthly phenomenon that neither of us has experienced. I'd say it's now or never. You have incredible legs. Have I told you that?"

She blushed, pleased as punch in spite of her protests. She had never been a lavish person before. But then, she'd never been to New York before. Looking at herself in the mirror, with Cameron behind her, engrossed now in fanning her hair over the fine silk fabric, she felt as though she'd fallen into a fairy tale. She had survived the flight and the harrowing ride from the airport, and now, in an entirely different world, she looked and felt like an entirely different person from the one who had left Pride just that day.

"I like the dress," she whispered, enchanted with the new woman she saw.

"Then we'll take it," he said and snapped his fingers for the saleswoman. While he was at it, he pointed to three other outfits, one more dressy and two less so, that he insisted on buying Summer. Her objections were overcome when they moved on to the men's department and the tables were turned. It was Cameron's turn to buy. Summer had seen him wearing jeans and a top, a towel, or nothing at all. She had never seen him in a slouchy blazer and pleated pants, or an exquisitely tailored suit that was nearly the same navy blue as his eyes. He was breathtakingly handsome in both, the fairy-tale prince to her princess.

And that was just the beginning. Dressed in the first of those new clothes—Summer in linen walking shorts, a matching blouse and blazer and wedge-heeled shoes, Cameron in khaki pants, a designer pullover and blazer—they walked down Fifth Avenue toward the hotel. Each time she saw her reflection in a store window, she looked twice.

*I can't believe that's me.*

*It's you. You're stunning.*

*And you. I can't believe that's us!*

His reflection sent her a satisfied grin. Shifting the bundles, he offered her an elbow, through which she promptly hooked her arm.

A suite was waiting at the Plaza in Cameron's name. If Summer had felt the city to be a different world, the accommodations were even more so. Standing just inside the door while the bellboy went through the motions of showing Cameron where everything was, she tried to take it all in, but each feature was more lush than the last. From the rich carpeting to the lavish bed covering and matching draperies, to the elegant love seat and side chairs, to the dressing table and desk, the room was exquisite, and that was before she dared peek at the magnificent bathroom.

"Like it?" Cameron asked, slipping his arms around her waist from behind.

She quickly turned and wrapped her own around his neck. "It's absolutely incredible. I love it."

"Not as overwhelming as you thought it would be?"

"Every *bit* so, but not frightening. I feel safe."

"With me."

She nodded and smiled. He could read the signs, could handle the airline tickets and the taxi fare, could register at the hotel—all things she would have had an awful time doing herself. And he was positively gorgeous, to boot.

He lowered his hands to the small of her back and pressed her hips close. His eyes darkened. His voice grew soft and grainy. "Y'know, I wouldn't care if we never opened the rest of these bundles. I wouldn't care if we stayed here naked all weekend."

"I would," she forced herself to say, though it wasn't entirely the truth. She felt a need to be naked with him right then, but there was another need she had. All her life she had been terrified of big, busy cities. Now she'd come to one, and the coming hadn't been painful at all. Yes, Cameron's presence was the key, but the result was the same. Her curiosity had been set free. She wanted to see more of New York.

"I hear you," he murmured resignedly. "But promise me something? Promise me that when we get back here later you'll let me look at you and touch you and hold you as much as I want." He tipped her chin up and caught her lips in a magnetic kiss. "Promise me," he said when he finally tore his mouth away, "that you'll touch me, too. This body is still a novelty to me. If I've only got it for a little while longer, I want to explore it more." His voice grew even softer. "Will you help me do that?"

Summer was starting to heat up from the inside out. "I'd like that," she said. Her eyes were on his mouth, then his neck, then his middle, which moved against hers less steadily than it had moments before. She put both hands there, spread her fingers over his tensing muscles. Unsure of what gave her the courage but unable to stop, she lowered them past his belt to the placket of his fly.

The sound of his moan was muffled against the crown of her head, where his mouth was pressed.

*You're so beautiful here,* she thought and moved her hands to explore his shape. *Even with clothes on, you're beautiful here.* She stroked the growing length of him, gently kneaded the heaviness beneath.

Another strangled sound came from above her. *Unzip me, sweetie. Touch me there. I think I'm dying.*

But she closed her eyes and retreated. Wrapping her arms around his waist, she held him tightly until she felt his muscles begin to relax. "Later," she promised and dared to look up. "One of the things about Earth bodies is that they thrive on temptation. The more excited they become without fulfillment, the more satisfying that fulfillment is when it finally comes."

He didn't look pleased. He was still partially erect.

She took a step back. "I've seen it happen on film. I want to know if it's so."

"You're cruel."

"Indulge me?"

Sighing, he ran a hand through his hair. "What men do in the name of love."

"You got that one right," she said with a grin and reached for the controls of the Jacuzzi.

SEVERAL HOURS LATER, after they had built up steam in the tub, worn it off with an ebullient walk down Broadway, then built it up again, they put on the most glamorous of their clothes and strode through the lobby of the Plaza to the front steps, where the doorman whistled them a cab.

"I'm someone else," Summer decided once she had settled into Cameron's arms in the backseat. "Summer VanVorn isn't doing this." Pride seemed a world away, her concern for it something distant and vague. In New York she was either a socialite or a movie star. More probably, she was the partner of one. Cameron was such a striking man that heads turned when they walked. He was confident, perfectly at ease, totally knowledgeable of cosmopolitan niceties such as greasing the ever-waiting palm. She was in awe of his urbanity. "Are you sure you haven't been here before?"

"I wouldn't lie about something like this," he said, and for an instant, watching him watch the passing glass, steel and stone, she saw the awe that gave credence to his words. "Films don't do it justice," he remarked. She agreed, all the more so when they arrived at the World Trade Center, took the elevator to the restaurant on top and were shown to a table overlooking the southern tip of Manhattan. The Statue of Liberty, so emblematic of all America stood for, was an inspiring glow in the night. Though Summer had never seen her before, as an American, she felt pride in showing her off to Cameron.

Dinner was every bit the dream that the rest of the day had been. Summer was unfamiliar with many of the things on the menu, but Cameron didn't have that problem. He ordered for them both, choosing a selection of unusual dishes, each of which was presented in an artistic fashion, each of which was delicious, as was the wine. She was feeling light and bright and airy by the time they descended to the ground floor and returned to the Plaza, but instead of leading her inside, Cameron took her up on her temptation theory and handed her into one of the horse-drawn carriages waiting nearby.

She didn't remember much of what they passed. The romance of the act blurred its details, while Cameron's nearness occupied her mind. She nestled into the crook of his shoulder, feeling protected and loved. She raised her face for his kiss, then held it there for another. She slid her hand over his shirt, rubbing her thumb back and forth over the wedge of hair that created texture through the fabric. She arched against him, needing his hands on her, too.

But he refrained from touching her where she ached. Instead, he stroked her neck, the hollow between her breasts, the inside of her wrist. He kissed her again and again, tasting her mouth, whispering his lips around, teasing her mercilessly. By the time they were in the lobby of the Plaza, a warm buzz was keeping her knees weak and her arm locked securely in his.

The door of their suite was barely shut when he pressed her to it and took her mouth in an avid kiss. She had never known a kiss could reach so deep and touch so many places, but like those spectacular eyes of his, Cameron's kiss did. It told her she was loved and desired. That knowledge increased her own love and desire tenfold.

Cameron started to tremble—a new, exciting and oddly disconcerting event—by the time he finally broke the suction of their lips. His voice was ragged. "Take off your clothes, sweetie. You promised."

She didn't need a promise to give her cause. Baring her body to him was natural and pleasurable. It was also necessary. She was beginning to feel that if his hands weren't on her soon, she would die of sheer frustration.

They separated, Summer going to the chair, Cameron to the desk.

Though the room was dark, the night outside was bright with city life. Above and beyond that neon reflection, the pale blue of a full moon lit their way. No words were spoken. The sound of traffic far below blended with the swish of clothing being removed and dropped, and the uneven sough of excited breathing. They watched each other undress, then when there was nothing left to remove, straightened and for the longest time simply admired each other's bodies.

Not once did it occur to Summer that, such a short time before, the thought of a man seeing her this way would have sent her into a defensive huddle. She felt no self-consciousness. The admiration in Cameron's eyes was vivid in the darkness, as was the rising state of his arousal.

His body entranced her. Her mind's eye traced his jaw, which bore the shadow of the beard that by rights he had to shave off twice daily. His neck was strong without being thick, his shoulders broad without being burly. Running an imagined hand over his chest was an exercise in adoration, a worshipful adventure over terrain that was manly and firm. She charted his contours, shaping her palms to muscular swells that leveled off as his body narrowed. His hips were lean, all lines leading to the spot where he was heavy and full for wanting her.

He swore in a gravelly voice. "And you think you lack the power? Keep on touching me like that, and I'll be done before we begin."

It was a minute before his words penetrated, and another minute before she could tear her eyes from the glory of his erection. "What?" she whispered.

"You were touching me with your mind. I felt your hands."

Dumbly she looked at those hands. They hung by her sides, yes, aching to touch him, but nearly ten feet away. *You felt these?*

*Like fire.*

Amazed, she let herself look at him again, this time imagining her palms skimming over the hair on his legs in a journey that took her ever upward to the point where those long legs met. There, growing bolder, she pictured her fingers around him, stroking the length of what looked to be hot, smooth silk.

"Summer . . ." he warned.

"Did you feel that?" she asked excitedly.

"Intimately."

She laughed in delight. Power was a heady thing. "And this?" She imagined the backs of her hands climbing his body, following the path of hair that began as a narrow line at his navel and flared into a wedge. She imagined the backs of those hands brushing lightly over his nipples, with devastating effect.

He put his shoulders back and made a sound of such pain that she was momentarily frightened. Running to him, she slid her arms around him and held him tightly. His heart hammered at the wall of his chest.

"I'm sorry," she murmured against his heated flesh. "It's just that I want to touch you so much."

Pushing his fingers into her hair, he lifted her face and seized her mouth with a hunger unlike any she'd ever felt in him. He didn't taste, he devoured. He ravaged every inch of the inside of her mouth, and when he was done, he ran his open mouth over her neck and throat, ever lower until she was bent back over his arm and he had taken her nipple into his mouth.

This time the agonized sound was hers. With her arms wrapped around his head, she held him closer. He suckled her. His teeth raked her. She began to shiver, clutching him to keep from falling.

As quickly as he had seized her, Cameron straightened. He hugged her for a steadying minute before lifting her in his arms and carrying her to the bed. With a flick of his wrist he threw back the blanket. After setting her on her knees, he reached for the lamp and put it on its lowest light. Then he was before her, lifting her until she straddled his hips.

He dropped his gaze to her breasts and caressed them with his eyes while his hands moved lower on her belly. When he looked there, she followed, and what she saw increased her shivers. His fingers were dark against the pale curls between her legs. The sight of them touched her even before they moved to prime her, but she didn't need priming, as those fingers quickly discovered. She was hot and moist in anticipation of his possession.

His eyes met hers. In a voice made gruff by need, he said, "Touch me now."

She did. He groaned in gratitude, but the reward was hers as much as his. He was hard, huge and heavy, made even more so by her rhythmic stroking—and the more aroused he grew, the more she wanted him inside. If the goal had originally been temptation, her limit was quickly reached. She couldn't imagine withstanding much more. She burned inside with wanting him.

*Now, Cameron!* she cried and slipped her arms around him. She felt his hands on her bottom, felt the start of his penetration, felt more of his sheathing, then more, until he was buried deeply inside her.

He sighed in relief, but the relief was short-lived. Summer felt it, too, that moment when so very much just wasn't enough. She fell back on the bed at his urging and raised her knees, then met his fierce thrusts with her own until the world began to spin, then tilt, then break apart in unfathomable pleasure.

THAT NIGHT was an endless succession of sex, talk and room-service delights. There were times when Summer felt she was at a pajama party, other times when she felt she was at an orgy. Having never been to either before, she wouldn't have dreamed of sleeping.

Come dawn, though, she lost her say in that. Pure exhaustion took over and held them both in its grip until well past ten. Loath to miss any more of the day, they showered, dressed and set out on foot. If the dearth of sleep had any effect, Summer, for one, didn't notice it. She had never felt so full of energy in her life.

They walked for miles, venturing to the very bottom of Fifth Avenue and exploring Washington Square and Greenwich Village, returning via the Empire State Building, Rockefeller Center, St. Patrick's Cathedral and Tiffany's. They bought hot dogs on one corner, frozen yogurt on another. From time to time they stopped to sit and watch the people walk quickly by.

"They look so intent on whatever they're thinking," Summer remarked during one of those stops. The words were no sooner out of her mouth when one of those intent passersby, a young man wearing a business suit and wing tips, dropped his briefcase. "Oops."

"Lucky for him it didn't open," Cameron said. "He'd be more panicked than intent if all the papers inside fell out."

"You wouldn't," she chided.

Innocently he held up both hands.

She looked at the staggered rows of people passing. Some were alone, some in pairs, some in threesomes. "I can't imagine anyone walking so quickly on Pride. Life there is so much slower."

"Do you feel stressed watching this?"

In response to the concern in his voice, she shot him a reassuring smile. "Oh, no. We're just visitors here. Besides, it's so exciting. New York is where things happen." She returned her gaze to the people. "I still can't believe I'm here."

He propped his weight on an arm behind her, bringing his body closer to hers. "Do you feel intimidated?"

She thought about that for a minute. All her life, it seemed, she had been intimidated by the world beyond

Pride. Yet she didn't feel it now. "It's your presence. You give me courage."

"No. Beyond that. Look at these women. Do you feel you're less important than they are?"

She thought about Pride, about the simplicity of her life there versus the complexity of these women's lives. "No," she said with a conviction that surprised even her. "I don't feel less important. They do their jobs and I do mine. From the looks of those somber faces," she mused, "I enjoy mine a lot more."

Just then, a woman approaching them at a mechanized clip glanced around. Her step didn't falter, but there was a curious look on her face as she went by. Soon after, a second woman did the same, and soon after that, a third.

"What did you do?" Summer asked when all three were safely past.

"Wolf-whistled in their ears."

"Cameron," she scolded.

He shrugged against her shoulder. "They should know that they're attractive, but they're in such a rush to get where they're going that I doubt they'd hear it if someone told them. Either that, or they'd turn around and smack the guy one."

"Do you think they're attractive?"

He looked at her. "Attractive, yes. As attractive as you, no. You're a breath of clean air, Summer."

She grinned. "*Fresh* air. A breath of fresh air."

He tossed off the difference with the crinkle of his nose. "Whatever it is, you are. I'd take you over them anyday."

Her grin stayed in place, hard put to fade when she was feeling so good inside. There was excitement about being in New York with Cameron. There was pride in the way she looked and, yes, in the attractive way she felt. There was astonishment that people weren't turning to stare at her; she was one of them, one of the crowd, and for a change, that was just fine. But there was something else that she felt, something new and still very tentative.

Power.

She had touched Cameron without touching him. Her mind had done the reaching and the feeling—at least, he claimed it had. She wondered if it was so.

Singling out an interesting man walking past, she imagined her hand on his shoulder. He looked around, saw no one, faced front and went on.

*A coincidence?* she wondered. Needing to know for sure, she found another man, this one dressed somewhat outlandishly in baggy pants, a silk shirt and wide suspenders. She set her mind to snapping the suspenders. Just at that moment, he turned away. She thought she saw him clap a hand over the suspenders, but she couldn't be sure.

So she tried it a final time. The man was a Kevin Costner look-alike, a little rough-hewn, a little sensitive, but compelling, particularly given the snugness of his jeans. In the time that she studied those jeans, he passed by. Knowing that he would soon be out of reach, she screwed up her courage and imagined her hand curving around his compact, denim-encased seat.

He whirled, eyes accusing every person within reach of him. They, in turn, marched blandly around him. Finally, red-faced, he continued down the street.

"That was daring," Cameron said.

"I did it!"

"You could have been more discreet."

"I wanted to know for sure."

"You could have picked someone ugly."

"But that's no fun!"

"Exactly," he muttered and drew her up and into step with the crowd once more. "Have I unleashed a sex maniac on the world?"

She laughed. No answer was necessary. Cameron knew that she loved him. As a reminder, she slipped her hand into the back pocket of his pants, craned her neck and kissed his ear. "Your bottom's the best one of all."

He seemed satisfied with that, because his step grew jaunty beside hers. Continuing past the Plaza, they went up Fifth Avenue to the Metropolitan Museum of Art. After two hours inside, they were ready for a rest. So they entered Central Park.

More than anything else she'd seen, this reminded her of home. Up until then, she had been busy enough and excited enough not to think about what might be happening on Pride. Sitting quietly with Cameron on one of the many benches beside the pond, though, her mind tripped helplessly back.

"Not to worry," Cameron assured her, ever attuned to her thoughts. "Everything's fine. The fellow from *People* may be there, but he won't get any information."

"What about someone else coming while we're gone?"

"The selectmen wouldn't dare do that. They wouldn't risk it."

She turned to him. "What do you *feel*? Anything happening there?"

Threading his fingers through hers, he shook his head. "Too far away. The power isn't that great. We may be remarkable, but we're not *that* remarkable." He suddenly grinned and pointed their fingers toward the far side of the pond. "Look. Isn't that little boy cute?"

Summer guessed the child to be no more than four years old. He was towheaded and tanned, wore a pair of short shorts and a T-shirt with a faded Ninja turtle on the front, and he was nudging a homemade sailboat out into the water.

"There's not much wind," she observed, wishing there were for the little boy's sake. Not far from his boat were two others, both larger and more elaborate than his, both clearly store-bought and expensive. Their owners were dressed accordingly.

Cameron slid his back lower against the bench and nonchalantly stretched out his legs. "Are they going to race?"

It looked that way to Summer. The three boys were talking to one another and pointing to their boats. After a minute, each retrieved his own, crouched low at the side of the pond and positioned it, then gave it a shove.

Sheer momentum carried the two heavier boats into the lead. They slowed gradually, but a tiny breeze kept them moving. Their owners, having already discounted the smaller, homemade boat, were crouching still, waving their hands, puffing out their cheeks and blowing, as though that would help fill the sails of their boats.

Suddenly there was movement around the homemade one. It rocked to one side, then to the other. Its sail filled, then flapped, filled, then flapped.

"What are you doing?" Cameron asked Summer under his breath.

"What are *you* doing?" she asked.

"I'm getting that boat going."

"So am I."

"Well, we're coming at it from opposite sides, so we're canceling each other out. Tell you what—you take the keel and hold it steady while I put some wind in the sails."

Summer didn't care who did what as long as the little boy won. She identified with him. He was the one of the three who was different. So she held the keel while Cameron filled the sails, and the homemade sailboat slipped through the water with just enough speed to overtake the other two.

"Faster," Summer urged.

"No, no," Cameron returned, concentrating. "Too fast and it'll look like a rout. Better it should be close." He grinned. "That's how Rocky always did it. Whoa, steady that keel," he commanded in nautical style.

The homemade boat reached the far shore barely a yard before the others. Dashing around the end of the pond as fast as his little legs would take him, the towheaded child caught it out of the water and, holding it high in glee, returned to the man Summer guessed to be his grandfather. The older man gave him a hug and hoisted him to his shoulder, which was how they left the park.

Summer sighed. "That was nice." But it was also poignant, even sad, for it made her think about the boy child Cameron said she carried. What a treat it would be to bring him here and let him win a race against fancier competition! But that would be four or five years from now. Cameron wouldn't be around then, and she couldn't come without him—not to mention the vague possibility that she wouldn't be around then, either.

"Vague?" Cameron asked.

She shrugged. "I'm trying to get used to the idea. It's taking a while."

"You have the power. You've proved that. Do you still doubt your ancestors were Cyteronian?"

"No. But what you're asking is extreme."

"I'm asking you to come home."

"Earth *is* home," she said, turning to him with a beseechful look. "Regardless of how much you've told me about Cyteron—" and they'd done more of that talking last night "—it's still foreign to me. This, on the other hand, is what I know."

"Not New York."

"Yes, New York. I've been hearing about it, watching shows and listening to tapes about it all my life. Everything here is familiar, certainly compared to Cyteron."

"But you couldn't live here."

"How do I know I can live on Cyteron?" It was the one question that kept cropping up, the one bound to disturb.

In response, he gave the one answer that could soothe. "Because you'd be with me. We'd be a pair." He nodded toward two ducks that were paddling around the pond. One was more brightly plumed than the other. They were clearly male and female. "That's how we'd be, rarely apart and then only briefly. We'd work together, raise our children together, play together. I want that, Summer." He brought her hand to his mouth. "I love you." He pressed his mouth to her palm.

With a soft sound of wanting, she ran her thumb over his firm lower lip. "I love you, too," she whispered, feeling it from head to toe.

"Then come with me."

"It's so frightening."

"It doesn't have to be, not if you trust me."

"I *do* trust you. But a different planet—a different solar system—a different galaxy—it's so strange."

Each time they had the discussion, it ended the same way. Summer made the one argument that Cameron couldn't deny. All he could do, which he did then, was to kiss her palm again, tuck it into his and draw her up from the bench and along on their way.

They went to Lincoln Center, but nothing was happening there to see. So they stopped in at the Museum of Natural History. When the exhibits failed to rivet them, they left and went to a movie. The highlight of that was the buttered popcorn they shared.

Back at the Plaza, they made love in the Jacuzzi, then climbed out, dried off and made love again in bed. And it was magic, the passion was. It enveloped them in its enchanted web, obliterating the image of the towheaded child at the pond. But the image returned, seeming symbolic of the dilemma Summer faced. For the life of her, she didn't know how to resolve it.

Cameron was as restless as she. He suggested that they dress, which they did, and have dinner at a deli on Sixth Avenue, which they did, and take a cab to the Limelight, an old church in the Village that had been converted into a disco, which they did. Unfortunately, neither of them knew how to dance. It wasn't something like sex, which you just *felt*, Cameron remarked and Summer agreed. Besides, the lights were too bright, the music too loud, the dance floor too small for the number of bodies it held. So they left.

"Are you feeling okay?" he asked her a short time later. They were at the Plaza, trying to decide what to do next.

"I guess," she said, but since that time at the pond, she hadn't been able to recapture the sense of abandon she'd felt before. "Kind of itchy."

"Yeah." He had his hands cocked on his Gucci belt and was looking past the revolving doors toward the east side of the city. His hair, so neatly combed when they had left earlier, fell rakishly over his brow but did nothing to soften his frown. "Like there's a storm brewing."

It struck her that he was right.

"Of course, I'm right," he said, but the look he gave her was less certain. "Think something's happening?"

She wasn't sure. On the one hand, the flush of her skin could well have been from the crush of the disco. Likewise, echoing the deafening beat of the music, the faint vibrating inside her. She touched Cameron's forearm, moved a finger over the hair there, but could she be sure that the sensitivity she felt was anything other than the awareness she always felt with him?

He took her hand and led her into the elevator. At their floor, he guided her down the hall. Once in the room, he drew her to the edge of the bed beside him and, remote control in hand, turned on the television—or tried. There was a minute of under-his-breath swearing before he pressed the right combination of buttons, and several minutes after that until he found the channel he wanted.

"...quickly gaining strength in the North Atlantic several hundred miles east of Bermuda," the weatherman was saying. "While it's still being called a tropical storm, we expect an upgrading to hurricane within the next few hours. This will be a storm to watch. If it continues on its current path, coastal areas from the Middle Atlantic states on up to Maine could be in for rough sailing."

Cameron looked at Summer. His eyes were the same dark blue as the water had been on that day, barely two weeks before, when she had been on the verge of drowning, only to be saved by the man who had so totally changed her life.

With quiet expectancy, he said, "So. We've come full circle."

# 11

THEY TOOK the first flight out of New York on Saturday morning, then a smaller plane from Portland to the mainland airfield closest to Pride.

"Storm's comin'," the pilot of the smaller plane told them. "Shouldn't hit us, though. One a season's 'bout all we ever get."

But Summer knew better. The feelings inside her—the vibration, the rise in temperature, the sensitivity—were stronger than ever and in Cameron, because of his Cyteron purity, even more so. His size made them easier to withstand, which explained how he had been able to swim strongly, storm and all, that first day. Still, she felt the heat of his skin and the vibrations that whispered from inside him. And then there was the issue of sensitivity to touch.

*This body sucks,* Cameron thought at one point and she didn't argue. Nor, though, did she take her hand from his. She needed to hold and be held, for what little comfort it could offer in the face of an ominous foreboding.

The sky was beginning to cloud over when they caught the ferry to Pride. "Expectin' some rain," the ferryman told them with a bored upward glance.

*Expectin' more than rain,* Cameron thought.

*When will it come?* Summer asked him.

*Twelve hours, no more. The feeling is intense. It'll be a big one.*

Summer felt the vibrations inside her increase—but these new ones were from fear, she knew. Her mother had always predicted a "big one." She had talked of a storm that would destroy the Isle of Pride, but over the years, when it hadn't come, Summer had chosen to put the warning down to exaggeration, as the rest of the islanders had done. Perhaps, though, her mother had been the one in the know. Cameron was certainly right about the feeling being intense. Summer couldn't remember feeling anything like this before.

By the time they reached Pride, the noon sun was hidden behind a blanket of gray clouds, beneath which an insistent breeze dotted the ocean with whitecaps. The ferry rocked nervously against the dock as they alighted. Their still stylishly clad feet had barely touched ground when a frazzled man approached the dock on the run. He was wearing a wrinkled white shirt tucked haphazardly into wrinkled denim shorts. A canvas bag bobbed on one shoulder; from the other rattled a bulging camera case and two cameras.

"Oh, no," Summer whispered. "The reporter." With so many more critical things on her mind during their premature return to Pride, she had forgotten that he would still be there.

But he rushed right on past them. "Big mistake," he warned as he went. "A hurricane's headed here. If you're smart, you'll turn around and take that ferry right back to the civilized world. Unless you like big winds. If so, stay, and I hope you get them. God knows there's nothing *else* of interest on this island." He bounded onto the ferry and disappeared into the sheltered cabin showing no interest in Summer and Cameron, whom he apparently took, from the fashionable clothes they wore, to be from the city.

They weren't about to hang around. Walking side by side at as fast a clip as Summer could manage, they left the dock and passed through the center of town. They didn't look to see who was watching them, but as they strode past the post office Millie waved from the door.

Summer ran to her.

"Storm's coming," Millie advised.

"I know." Summer touched the older woman's shoulders and spoke loudly. She didn't care who else heard, as long as Millie did. "It's going to be a bad one. Have you somewhere safe to go?"

"My cottage is good as iron."

"No. Safer."

Millie frowned. "T'won't be that bad. You're sounding like your mama now."

"You have a root cellar, don't you?"

"Yes, but—"

"When the winds get bad, go there, Millie. Promise me you will."

"I will, but—"

Summer gave the woman a quick, awkward hug and ran to join Cameron. She didn't look back. She didn't want to consider the fact that she might never see Millie again.

By unspoken agreement, they went to the meadow first. Dropping the bags she carried, Summer breathed a sigh of relief when she saw the ponies. She counted them; they were all there. She walked into their midst, greeting each.

"They feel it, too," she told Cameron, who was close behind her.

"Yes."

She raised frightened eyes to his. "What do we do?"

Calmly he said, "We try to secure the cabin. Then we wait."

"There?"

"Here."

She nodded, bade the ponies a temporary goodbye and retrieved her bags.

The cabin was as it had been when they'd left it two days before. If anyone had entered and explored in their absence, there was no sign of the intrusion. Not that it mattered. Life had changed for Summer. Deep inside, she sensed that the old order was on its way out. And the new order? What was it? She didn't know! She just didn't know!

Attuned to her bewilderment, Cameron took her in his arms and held her tightly. He didn't say anything, just held her, letting the strength of his body speak for itself.

Outside, the wind began to gust through the trees. Its menacing howl brought her head up. "There are boards in the back shed. Should we nail them over the windows?"

"We could."

She read something else in his words. "But it won't do much good."

He shook his head. "If the wind comes the way I'm feeling it will, everything goes."

She swallowed the knot that rose in her throat. "The cabin?" He nodded. "The beech trees?" He confirmed that, too. "The *ponies*?"

"Everything."

"What about you?" she asked and held her breath.

The navy in his eyes grew deep and rich. Behind it, the look that had always been so familiar cried out to her. "Me, too. It's time."

Her breath escaped her in an agonized cry. She began to shake. "Now?"

"Soon." His arms went around her, but no matter how tightly he held her—or she held him—her shaking went on.

"What do I do?" she cried.

"Come with me."

"I can't."

"Yes, you can."

"I'm an Earth thing."

"Only in part."

"But that part will keep me here."

"Not if you want to go."

"But I don't know *how* to go!"

He took her face in his hands. There was an urgency in his fingers consistent with the fierce expression in his eyes. "You will when the time comes. All you have to do is want it."

*I want it. I don't. I want it. I don't.*

He held her again. She clung to his shirt, his back, his neck. Eyes squeezed shut, she tried to imagine a life without him, but couldn't. He was her completion, the key to who she was. She could never be whole again without him.

The wind grew louder, then louder still. When the cabin walls reverberated with it, Cameron drew back and looked at her. "I have to go to the meadow."

Tears sprang to her eyes. The moment of truth was approaching, but she needed more time!

"Now," he said softly.

Brushing at her tears with the back of her hand, she clung to his arm. At the door, she looked back and her tears welled again.

"You'll always have this, you know," he said. "It'll always be in your mind, right along with the memories. And you'll have so much more."

She wanted to believe him, wanted to believe him *so badly*, but she was human, with a wealth of human doubts and fears.

"Come on," he whispered and led her out into the wind.

They fought their way up the slope behind the cabin and took the path through the woods. The pines swayed madly above them, sweeping the sky and each other with increasing force. By the time they reached the meadow, it was raining, large drops that came more steadily with each minute that passed.

As oblivious to the rain as she was, Cameron sat down on the old tree stump and drew her onto his lap. With an arm wrapped tightly around his neck, she watched the ponies move from beech tree to beech tree. They weren't eating. Summer guessed they were too unsettled. It was almost as though they were saying goodbye.

Completing the circle of Cameron's neck with her other arm, she buried her face in his hair and started to cry.

"Don't, sweetie," he said in a tortured voice. "They'll be fine. So will you."

Still her tears came. *I love you.*

His arms tightened around her. *Then you'll come.*

*But can I?* She had asked the question dozens of times. Still she didn't know the answer.

*You can if you believe.*

*Believe in what?*

*In me. In us.*

*I do!*

*Then think yourself with me.*

She was wondering how to do that when a vicious gust of wind shook Cameron's body. He slid to the ground and used the tree stump for support, but he had no sooner secured Summer when a yawing sound brought their heads up fast.

In a motion so slow as to be nearly unreal, one of the beeches keeled over, its roots torn from the meadow soil.

"No," Summer cried, pushing her wet hair from her eyes. "Oh, no." She would have run to the tree in a frantic attempt to right it had Cameron not been holding her fast. "I have to help," she protested, raising her voice over the wind and rain.

"There's nothing you can do. You'll only be hurt if you try." There was another yawing sound, and another tree fell.

Cameron got to his feet.

"*No!*" she screamed and clung to him, but he broke away. Pressing a trembling hand to her mouth, she watched him go to the ponies. Their silver heads came up at his approach, their eyes filled with what Summer would have said was relief, if she trusted her own eyes. But they were awash with tears. It seemed the whole *world* was awash with tears, everything wet, everything swimming.

That was why, when the first of the ponies disappeared, she put it down to faulty vision. When the second and third disappeared, she blinked, but by the time half of the herd was gone, she was staring in astonishment. All it took was his touch, it seemed. He extended a gentle caress and, on contact with his hand, one pony after the next grew blindingly white, then shrank to a brilliant dot and soared off into the wind. Again and again it happened, until there was one pony left.

Pumpkin.

Man and horse came toward her through the wind and the rain. "He won't listen to me," Cameron shouted. "You'll have to tell him. If he stays he'll die."

She could see that now. More of the beeches had been felled by the wind. They would all be gone before long, leaving nothing for even a single pony to eat.

Tears ran down her face. *Go, Pumpkin!* she cried. *Be safe!*

"Touch him," Cameron told her, leading the horse closer. "He needs to feel your conviction."

"My conviction. Oh, God."

A pine limb fell not five feet from them. "Hurry, sweetie."

Summer reached out, then drew her hands back. She wanted to touch the pony, wanted it desperately, but for the very last time?

"He'll die," Cameron reminded her. "You've spent your life tending him. Don't let him down now."

She touched Pumpkin's forelock. *Join the others! Be healthy and alive!* "Go, Pumpkin!" Her scream was swallowed by the storm, but her hand was suddenly warm, her eyes blinded. In the next instant, she was touching air.

Bewildered, she turned to Cameron. He was drenched—his dark hair in spikes on his brow, his tanned skin streaked with rain, his clothing sodden. He looked as beautiful as she'd ever seen him, but the beauty was from within as much as without. He was a man of gentleness and caring, and she loved him for that. She loved his wit, his sense of adventure, his courage. She loved him for the vulnerability that she saw just then in his eyes.

"What'll it be?" he asked, lowering his mouth in a desperate kiss. Her lips clung to his until he forced a break. "Come with me," he begged. The desperation had spread

to his voice and his eyes. "It's a better world, Summer.
You'll be happy, healthy and safe. I know you're frightened because it's so different from what you've known,
but if you trust me, you'll know that what I say is true.
You're a brave woman. You've had to be brave, living
here, and that bravery will stand by you wherever you
go." He gave her a tiny shake. "I want you to come with
me. I've never loved before, and I never will again. It's
you or nothing. Come with me, Summer."

She touched his face, giving her frantic fingertips a final feel of his stubbled jaw, his square chin, his straight
nose. "I want to," she sobbed. "I want to." Her hands
went to his broad shoulders, then down his long arms.
"But I don't know how!"

He took her face in his hands and held it so tightly she
could barely breathe. His eyes were bright behind their
navy blue. As he spoke, a halo emerged behind his head.
"Think trust. Think power. Think love. They're inter-
twined. If you believe in all three, you're with me."

Gone from Earth. Off into space. Changed in form
forever.

"I want to believe," she cried and, terrified, watched
the halo spread to his shoulders.

"Then *do* it," he urged. "Do it *now*."

His mouth formed the words, but the sound came from
somewhere else, because a blinding light had suddenly
taken the place of his body, and in the next instant the
light was a shimmering star and he was gone.

Deprived of his support, she staggered. "Cameron?"
She whirled around. "Cameron!" He was nowhere to be
seen amid the ravaged trees and the rising puddles.
"*Cameron!*" she screamed, doubling over with the effort.

*Believe me, Summer.*

"Where *are* you?" she sobbed.

*Think trust. Think power. Think love. Close your eyes, and believe in us. Come with me, sweetie. I need you.*

"I need you, too!" she cried and realized how very true it was. As frightened as she was of going to Cyteron, she was more frightened of remaining on Earth without Cameron. He was her sun, the center of her universe. Without him she would wander, aimless and cold. But she didn't want that. She wanted to see her mother again. She wanted her son to know both his parents. She wanted to love Cameron for the hundreds of years he had promised.

If joining him meant the end of the past, so be it. Without him the future was bleak.

Strengthened by a new resolve, she straightened, raised her face to the rain and closed her eyes. "I believe," she whispered and put her trust in Cameron to bring her safely to him. "I believe," she said more loudly and garnered her own power to aid in the trip. "I believe!" she cried fervently and gave herself up to love.

Suddenly a blissful warmth spread through her body. It took the weight of worry from her shoulders, leaving her light as air and alive with excitement. For a split second she thought Cameron was making love to her—the rush of adrenaline was the same. But the pleasure she felt was even more elemental. Her body was purified, then liquefied, made beautiful in a world that was at once soft and luminous.

*I'm coming, Cameron!* she thought with a victorious smile, and, in a flash of radiance, she was gone.

# Epilogue

MILLIE OSGOOD AWOKE as always with the sun and, struggling to overcome the stiffness in her arthritic bones, bathed and dressed. Taking a bag of birdseed from the kitchen cupboard, she made her slow way to the back porch and filled the tiered feeder that hung from the porch overhang. Just as she finished, a small movement caught her eye. She looked across the rutted path toward the large oak a short distance away.

From behind it, a figure emerged. She was petite, with dark hair that was cut short in the popular boy's style, but not for a minute did Millie think she was either a child or male. Wearing a poet's shirt over slim jeans, she was definitely a young woman, looking sweet and innocent, even a little frightened.

Enchanted, Millie gestured her forward. When she took a single step and stopped, the postmistress gestured again. This time, albeit tentatively, she kept coming. Several feet away, she stopped.

"I was just about to make my morning tea," Millie said. "Can I offer you some?"

She shook her head, then gave a shy smile, and in a voice that was as shy as the smile and almost too soft for Millie to hear, she said, "No. Thank you."

Millie studied her. She appeared new and fresh, really quite lovely. She also looked familiar. With a frown that further furrowed her wrinkled brow, Millie asked, "Have we met before?"

"No," the woman said, still softly and shyly.

"You look like...you look like..." Millie struggled to make the comparison, but at eighty-four her brain was dusty. "No matter, I s'pose. You're certainly a pretty sight around here, and so early in the morning. I didn't see you in town yesterday. You must have come in late."

"I came this morning."

"Oh, but it's much too early for the ferry."

"I sailed."

"Did you now?" Millie said in admiration. To be sailing before dawn was quite something, given the moodiness of the North Atlantic around Pride. "You're an adventurous one. What's your name?"

"Dahlia."

Millie thought the name was as lovely as the woman. It wasn't often that people with culture arrived on Pride, and this Dahlia clearly had it. There was a refinement to her. No doubt she was well-educated. "Dahlia what?"

"Monroe."

That got Millie to struggling with her memory again. "There were some folks named Monroe here a while back. Any relation?"

With an apologetic look, Dahlia shook her head.

"Now that's no problem," Millie cooed with a crinkly smile. "They weren't the best of sorts, if you know what I mean." She didn't know if Dahlia did, because rather than respond, she was reaching under her shirt into the back pocket of her jeans.

"I have something for you." She handed over a small muslin pouch.

Millie recognized it instantly. She hadn't seen a pouch like it since Summer VanVorn had left, and had missed it dearly. "Tea?" she asked eagerly.

Dahlia nodded. "Summer sent it. She said it would help your arthritis."

"It certainly will, but tell me, child, have you seen Summer? I haven't heard a word from her since that terrible storm we had, and that was nearly two years ago now. She saved my life, you know. If it'd been up to me, I'd have stayed in this cottage during the storm, but my roof caved in and would've killed me if I'd done that. No, I was in the root cellar, just where she told me to go. How *is* Summer?"

"She's fine. She sends her love. And this, too." Reaching into a pocket on her other side, she drew out a second pouch.

Millie peeked inside and her face broke into a delighted smile. "She remembered. What a dear she is. Why, I was telling her how much I loved these candies, not more'n a few days before she left. Her mother used to make them. Her grandmother, too. Summer must have remembered the recipe after all. Tell me, where is she living?"

"Up north. She's married now. She and Cameron have a little boy. He's such a beautiful little thing. He positively sparkles. They all do. They're very happy."

Millie heard the business about a little boy, but missed what followed. She cupped her ear. "Come again?"

"They're very happy," Dahlia said more loudly.

"Is she still a healer?"

"Not so much now. She's very devoted to her family. She goes everywhere with Cameron. The baby comes, too. There's even a second one on the way, a little girl this time."

"My, my, how clever it is that folks nowadays know whether it's a boy or a girl before it's born. We used to have to take our chances. But isn't that exciting news about Summer. I always felt badly for her being so alone and all. I was happy when her young man came along." She frowned, studying Dahlia more closely. "Maybe that's it. You have his eyes. It's not many people who have navy blue eyes like that. They're quite striking." But she wasn't sure it was the eyes. There was something else. Distractedly, because she was trying to identify that something else, she said, "We miss her here. Oh, the others will never admit it in so many words, but Summer did us a service with her skill. Anyone who's sick now has to go to the mainland, and that's not so easy sometimes. Pride needs a person like Summer who knows about roots and herbs and things like that."

"I know about them," Dahlia said softly.

"Do you now? But surely you're just passing through."

"Actually I've been looking for a quiet place to live. Summer spoke highly of Pride. I may explore the idea."

"You won't find things like they were in Summer's time," Millie cautioned sadly. "The meadow she loved so was destroyed in the hurricane. Isn't nothing but mud now. Nothing seems to want to grow there, and the ponies haven't been back, either. Did Summer tell you about them?"

Dahlia nodded.

Millie sighed. "They were something to see, all gray and misty. In a certain light, you'd'a thought they were ghosts." Her eyes lit up. "That's it. You look just like that little girl in the movies. You know, the one whose young man turns into a ghost. What was her name?" She pushed at her forehead with a gnarled finger, trying to shake things up a bit. "What was her name? It was

a strange one—not Tammy—Demi—Demi Moore."
Pleased as punch with herself, she said, "I'm the post-
mistress here. Have been for as many years as anyone can
remember, so I know my names. Demi Moore's the one
I wanted. You look just like her with your short dark hair
and that haunted look. Of course, the eyes are different.
If the lady in the movie had eyes like that, I'd've noticed.
They're unusual eyes."

"They run in my family," Dahlia said.

"And where is your family, may I ask?"

Dahlia gestured toward the distant horizon.

"And you traveling around all alone? You're too sweet
to be all alone. I wouldn't be alone if I didn't have to, but
my Angus died some thirty years ago, and by then all the
men on the island were taken. So I keep myself busy with
my work and my books and my birds, and there's folks
who drop in to see me. It's nice." It was nice, nice and
predictable, and sometimes boring, which was one of the
reasons she had always liked seeing the VanVorn women
around. She missed having Summer drop by. Summer
had been the sweetest of all.

Feeling suddenly lonesome and older than she had
moments before, she said to Dahlia, "Are you sure you
won't come in for a cup of tea? I would truly like the
company."

Dahlia started to shake her head, then stopped. Millie
could see her wavering.

"Come," she urged, opening the door to the kitchen.
"Come tell me about Summer. If you do," she added with
a twinkle in her faded eyes, "I'll give you all the island
news to send back. I'll even tell you about the little cottage that just went up for sale on the bluff. It's a tiny
thing, but it has a special charm. You just may like it."

Still, Dahlia hesitated.

"Folks around here aren't big on thank yous," Millie said, "but you've just given me two special gifts, and you've given me word on Summer. How can I thank you if not by having you in my house?"

"Are you sure?" Dahlia asked, looking cautiously around.

Millie's neighbors were still sleeping, and even if they weren't, Millie didn't care. Since Summer VanVorn had saved her life, she'd grown bold about certain things. "I have in my house who I want, and I want you. Come, Dahlia. I'm ready for a cup of Summer's tea."

Dahlia hesitated for just a moment longer before preceding her inside.

# A NOTE FROM BARBARA DELINSKY

After writing as many Temptation novels as I have, the challenge becomes writing a story that is fresh and new. Cameron Divine is about as fresh and new a hero as I've created. He is strong, insightful and larger than life, a captivating blend of reality and fantasy, snagging my heart when he first scooped Summer from the sea and holding it through to the very last page.

Cameron's story offers something I believe we all need from time to time. He has explanations for the inexplicable. Lord, how I wish I could understand my own personal limitations in as rational a manner as Cameron understands Summer's and his own!

Yet, *The Outsider* isn't a one-sided story. As special as he is, Cameron doesn't come to the Isle of Pride looking for love. It is Summer who wakes him up to the most basic of all human emotions and offers him the experience of *his* life.

*The Outsider* is about dreams, about letting the imagination run wild, about believing in the unbelievable. It is about liberal-mindedness, about rising above the norm and opening ourselves to new ways of thinking. If nothing else, I wish this for my readers.

# HARLEQUIN Temptation

## Rebels & Rogues

All men are not created equal. Some are rough around the edges. Tough-minded but tenderhearted. Incredibly sexy. The tempting fulfillment of every woman's fantasy.

When it's time to fight for what they believe in, to win that special woman, our Rebels and Rogues are heroes at heart. Twelve Rebels and Rogues, one each month in 1992, only at Temptation!

**Jake:** He was a rebel with a cause, but a beautiful woman threatened it all.

**THE WOLF** by Madeline Harper.
Temptation #389, April.

If you missed the previous Rebel and Rogue titles, THE PRIVATE EYE (#377), THE HOOD (#381) or THE OUTSIDER (#385), and would like to order them, send your name, address, zip or postal code, along with a check or money order for $2.99 plus 75¢ postage and handling ($1.00 in Canada) for each book ordered, payable to Harlequin Reader Service to:

| In the U.S. | In Canada |
|---|---|
| 3010 Walden Avenue | P.O. Box 609 |
| P.O. Box 1325 | Fort Erie, Ontario |
| Buffalo, NY 14269-1325 | L2A 5X3 |

Please specify book title(s) with your order.
Canadian residents add applicable federal and provincial taxes.

RR-4

# Take 4 bestselling love stories FREE

## Plus get a FREE surprise gift!

## Special Limited-time Offer

### Mail to Harlequin Reader Service®

| In the U.S. | In Canada |
|---|---|
| 3010 Walden Avenue | P.O. Box 609 |
| P.O. Box 1867 | Fort Erie, Ontario |
| Buffalo, N.Y. 14269-1867 | L2A 5X3 |

**YES!** Please send me 4 free Harlequin Temptation® novels and my free surprise gift. Then send me 4 brand-new novels every month, which I will receive before they appear in bookstores. Bill me at the low price of $2.69* each—a savings of 30¢ apiece off the cover prices. There are no shipping, handling or other hidden costs. I understand that accepting the books and gift places me under no obligation ever to buy any books. I can always return a shipment and cancel at any time. Even if I never buy another book from Harlequin, the 4 free books and the surprise gift are mine to keep forever.

*Offer slightly different in Canada—$2.69 per book plus 49¢ per shipment for delivery. Canadian residents add applicable federal and provincial sales tax. Sales tax applicable in N.Y.

142 BPA ADL4                                            342 BPA ADMJ

_____
Name                          (PLEASE PRINT)

_____
Address                                   Apt. No.

_____
City                    State/Prov.              Zip/Postal Code.

This offer is limited to one order per household and not valid to present Harlequin Temptation® subscribers. Terms and prices are subject to change.

TEMP-92                                © 1990 Harlequin Enterprises Limited